Praise for *A Room*

T0083278

"*A Room of Rain* is a group of seamless short stories by an old master of the form. Gary Fincke has never hesitated to ask hard questions in his work, and these stories are determined to take the toughest situations by the horns."

—Madison Smartt Bell, author of twelve novels, including the Haitian Revolutionary trilogy of *All Souls' Rising, Master of the Crossroads*, and *The Stone That The Builder Refused*

"For years, Gary Fincke has quietly built a reputation as one of the nation's finest storytellers. This glorious collection shows him at the peak of his powers—funny, gritty, provocative."

—Cary Holladay, author of *The Deer in the Mirror*

"Gary Fincke is one of the most reliable and prolific writers out there, and *A Room of Rain* is clearly one of his strongest collections. In this world that seems so quick to stick labels on everything, Fincke goes around ripping off all the stickers. He convincingly blurs the line between what is taboo and what is not, refusing to allow readers to back away into safety; these stories illustrate the notion that we all have taboo thoughts, that beneath the surface, none of us are 'ordinary,' none of us 'pure.' At his best, he reminds me of Richard Yates—Fincke flat out knows how to write."

—Jim Daniels, author of *Eight Mile High* and other collections

"This collection is provocative yet subtle; gritty yet humorous. The characters are round and the short stories are complete, though often feel like the tip of an iceberg. I wanted more because of how drawn I was to the characters, not because the tales left me unsatisfied. These stories continue to stick with me long after closing the book, beautifully rendered reminders of what we each hold untold."

—Genevieve Shifke Ali, *Independent Publisher*

A ROOM OF RAIN

GARY FINCKE

A Room
of Rain

STORIES

VANDALIA PRESS
MORGANTOWN 2015

West Virginia University Press 26506

Copyright 2015 West Virginia University Press / Vandalia Press

Vandalia Press is an imprint of West Virginia University Press

All rights reserved

First edition published 2015 by West Virginia University Press

Printed in the United States of America

22 21 20 19 18 17 16 15   1 2 3 4 5 6 7 8 9

ISBN

Paper: 978-1-940425-20-7

EPUB: 978-1-940425-22-1

PDF: 978-1-940425-21-4

Cataloguing-in-Publication data is available at the Library of Congress.

Book and cover design by Than Saffel; Cover llustration by Jeffrey A. Bland.

The individual chapters of this book have been previously published as follows: "A Room of Rain," *The Journal* (Pushcart nominee); "The Worst Thing," *The Missouri Review*; "Isn't She Something?" *Sonora Review* (Best American Short Stories citation); "The Comfort of Taboos," *Pleiades* (Pushcart Prize citation); "The Visual Equivalent of Pain," *The Kenyon Review*; "After Arson," *Newsday* (PEN Fiction Prize); "All Square," *Cimarron Review*; "Household Hints," *Beloit Fiction Journal*; "Saints," *Santa Monica Review*; "Perfect," *Southern California Review*; "Roger That," *Crazyhorse.*

As always, to Derek, Shannon, Aaron, and especially Liz.

CONTENTS

A ROOM OF RAIN

"YOU COME AWAY FROM THAT television set and watch this show right here in your own backyard," my mother shouted through the screen of the open living room window, but I waited until the commercials came on before I went outside.

"What show?" I said when I reached the back porch. I couldn't make out anything special because it was raining, a drizzle, the kind that I walked in fifty times a year without an umbrella while she lectured me about how I'd have pneumonia before I knew what hit me.

There she was, standing in it, her hands out to the side like she was a little girl who had the day off school, like I did, for Veteran's Day. "Come over here beside me, Bradley," she said, using my full name like she did when she wanted me to know the words were important. I didn't mind. The rain, thin and soft, felt good. "Isn't this the cat's meow?" she said, but after a few seconds I was thinking about how the commercials would be over in a minute, maybe less, while she took my hand and said, "I have a surprise for you." And she walked me, I swear, just seven steps before the sun came out. There wasn't a cloud in the sky. Not one.

"Well?" she said, and I ran back into the drizzle and then out on another side, only six steps until I was in the sun again and could see around the edge of it to where she was standing. It was raining only in our yard, and not even the whole yard at that, just the part up against the back porch on the side next to the Daigenaults' house.

I know what you're likely thinking, getting ready to go back to your own television shows, but even now, fifty years later, you can find our rain mentioned in those books full of lists of the biggest and smallest and oddest things to ever happen to anybody on this earth. The World's Smallest Rain—there we are because we ended up with the witnesses you need because while we walked around that rain, my mother told me she'd already called the airport, where somebody was always interested in the weather. "You had your nose glued to that TV, but I kept watching out the kitchen window while I talked to them to make sure it hadn't stopped. They're on their way. It took some convincing, let me tell you. It was easier to get you out here away from the television."

She had her camera, too, the little Kodak she kept handy by the phone "just in case," and she told me to stand inside the rain. "Now outside," she said, and I positioned myself with one foot in and one foot out as she laughed and snapped away before she stepped back and took the whole thing in from the Daigenaults' yard.

We had ourselves a room of rain outside. And it lasted for more than two hours, long enough for the weather people from the airport to examine that shower for almost an hour before it dried up and let the sun shine on all of our yard, including that small, damp part as big as our kitchen.

"Aren't you glad you listened to your mother?" she said when it was all over.

"Yes."

"A boy who didn't listen would have stayed glued to the television and missed the whole thing."

I thought about the old movie I was watching when she called, the dad from *Father Knows Best* all made up a long time ago to look like he'd been burned and scarred. He was supposed to be a World War II veteran, and by the time my mother called me outside, I could see what was happening, he and this homely woman going to a cottage where they turned better looking when they were inside. I wanted to know how it all worked out, whether they stayed inside that little house the rest of their lives in order to look handsome and beautiful or if they really knew they hadn't changed at all.

The weather people decided the small rain was somehow connected to the air conditioner in the Daigenaults' house, but they didn't say how, and there was no way to prove themselves right except them saying, "What else could it have been?"

"A miracle," my mother said. "A sign." But just like the weather people, she couldn't prove it unless something strange happened or the rain came back in a different part of the yard.

She watched the yard the next day. She tried not to let on, but I saw my mother leaning over the sink to look out before I left for school and, that night, how she kept herself in the chair she never used because it sat in bad light for reading in order to face the back window in the living room.

Me? I switched on the television because I didn't expect something so weird to happen twice. If nobody had ever heard of such a thing, it wasn't going to happen again anytime soon. And if it did, a tiny rain like that, and it fell somewhere else, that would ruin it, like a new set of quintuplets getting born and all of them living. Nobody would care about another batch like the ones in Canada my mother and father had gone to see just before my sister Eileen was born, holding me up to look at all five dressed the same in Quintland, the place where they came out to play while people watched. My mother talked about them so much that when I was in first grade, I asked to go back so I could see them again with Eileen. "They're not being shown anymore," she said. "You'll just have to remember as best you can."

My father believed in the weathermen. "The Daigenaults," he said, "they're always running that air conditioner of theirs like it would kill them to break a sweat, and here it is November and Armistice Day already, and we're not at the equator here even if snow would be a surprise in January. You mess with your weather long enough, you start to get the world into wrongness."

"Veterans Day, Bob," my mother said. "They changed the name four years ago."

"You can't change something by calling it a new name," my father said. He never complained about how hot it was when we moved south just over a year ago. He knew my mother wanted an air conditioner. She'd lived her whole life, like all of us, up by Cleveland, and she wasn't anywhere near being used to Louisiana.

"There's no way that bitty thing could make it rain for hours."

"Who did? God?"

"Maybe so," she said. "Maybe we've been picked out for a special something we need to be ready for."

"You keep wishing, Gladys," he said. "Next thing you know we'll be in heaven."

She looked at me. I'd stopped eating. "Bradley stood in that rain with me," she said. "If you'd gotten wet, you wouldn't talk like that."

"I believe that part, Gladys. But you didn't see God. I know that for a fact. The Daigenaults don't even go to our church."

When the television station called my mother and said they wanted to film her standing in our backyard, I asked to stay home from school, but my father took me down the hall before he told me, "Absolutely not." My mother didn't follow us. "This isn't a good thing, Brad," my father said. He was knotting his tie, tugging so hard I thought he could choke himself.

"Being on television is the coolest thing in the world."

"Never mind what you think. You ponder what I've said for a minute and you'll see." He tugged the knot, centering it between the tips of his collar before he buttoned them down. "All harnessed up," he said while I counted seconds in my head, but he started to leave just before I reached twenty-two, so I quicksaid, "It's been a minute, and I don't see what's wrong."

He laid his hands on my shoulders and squeezed while I stared at the blue tie that split his pressed white shirt. "Then you'll just have to watch and learn."

That night, after I'd told my teachers at school to stay up late to get a look at my mother on the news at eleven o'clock, I settled down beside her to watch while my father sat in a chair off to the side where he could see without looking like he was paying attention. "An unusual story this evening," the anchorman said at 11:28. The segment was right at the end, after the sports and the weather. "The Last Word," they called it. On the screen my mother was standing exactly where the rain fell, and she held out her hands the way she had, looking up like she expected the rain to begin. "It was real, all right," she said. "The weather people came and saw it all before it went away."

They showed the Daigenaults' air conditioner unit where it sat next to their house. "Conditions appear to have been perfect for a man-made shower," the announcer said as she looked up at the sky for a moment. "This is Ellen Garleaux for 'The Last Word.' Good night."

My mother was angry. "I told them that wasn't true," she said. "I talked to them for fifteen minutes and said how you could see the rain didn't reach to the Daigenaults'. I showed them my pictures as proof and said it was a sign of something we just had to wait for."

"It was good," my father said, and I knew right off what he meant by that.

"Good I got fifteen seconds for seeing such a thing? And not a mention of me talking about Brad. I even mentioned you."

"Even better then they shut you up the way they do."

"You know what I wish about all this?" she said then, and when my father didn't speak, I said, "What?"

"That Eileen had lived to see that rain. She'd have laid herself right down on that grass and let it soak right in. She'd have thought it was a dream come true."

My sister Eileen had been a Comet-Girl. Twice a week she went to Gym-Starz in Cleveland, where a woman who once had been the second alternate on an Olympic team trained girls and boys to flip and tumble and balance in ways that frightened me and my mother but thrilled my father. He'd signed her up before she started kindergarten because, he said, "She's a natural."

I'd seen Eileen do cartwheels like other little girls, but my father was impressed by the way she danced with him when he played the jive music he loved. As soon as Eileen heard Louis Prima or Cab Calloway, she ran to his arms and he'd lift her over his head while she squealed and shrieked, jumping, jiving, and wailing like Louis Prima himself was twirling her. My father would toss her up and catch her. He'd swing her in a circle, her legs outstretched so her body was nearly parallel to the floor, and when he was exhausted, she'd ask to do it again.

There were only a few boys among the dozens of girls at Gym-Starz. The ones Eileen's age were called Meteor-Boyz. If I had been different when I was four, my father might have signed me up, but by that time I already grew tense as soon as he lifted me, and my fear made me cling to him. "He's so careful," I heard my father telling my mother, the word sounding like "stupid" when he said it.

For a few weeks he asked me to relax, and then he didn't ask, dancing alone with a bottle of beer in his hand, my mother long ago letting him know she wasn't interested in any dancing except where two people held each other close and moved slowly to songs about love's joys and heartaches. Maybe five nights he danced by himself before Eileen, almost two, began to beg him to throw her around.

"There were good times before our troubles," my mother would say. "You have to remember that."

I always acted like I did, but back then, even though my father traveled less and Eileen was there, seven years old, I remembered how there weren't any visitors but grandparents. Nobody my parents' age ever sat on the living room furniture.

I'd visit my friends and imagine their mothers and fathers coming to our house for dinner, what they would talk about while we ate. That last summer in Cleveland, it would have been the *Andrea Doria* colliding with another ship and all those passengers drowning when it sank. Or Egypt taking over the Suez Canal and acting like they wanted to start a war, both things happening near the end of July.

Those news items were on television, and my mother watched the early edition at ten o'clock the nights my father was on the road somewhere. She let me stay up because it was summer, but Eileen had to be in bed by nine. She said, "This is for grown-ups. Are you big enough to watch?" and I would sit beside her hoping this would be one of those nights when she wouldn't turn it off after the sports and weather, an old movie keeping us on the couch until midnight.

It was August 1 when Eileen drowned, and the television didn't come on again until September when we moved. Whatever happened with the Suez Canal took care of itself without us knowing about it because we didn't get a newspaper, and there wasn't even a radio in our car. The house was so quiet I started talking to myself out loud, the grass nobody cut for a month up past my ankles, the pool turning as algae-filled as the scum-covered pond at the end of our street.

All those people on the *Andrea Doria* who'd drowned? I wondered if they were at the bottom of the ocean or if somebody had pulled them up like my mother had done for Eileen.

"My sister is dead." I said that sentence to myself every day for weeks, but as soon as we moved, I didn't say it anymore, and it was like I'd never had a sister except when I saw her clothes hanging in the closet in the room next to mine. Each time some strange boy or girl in my new school asked me if I had any brothers or sisters, I said, "No," and it was true.

My mother, a month after we moved to Louisiana, began to sleep in the room that Eileen would have used. "It's just gathering dust," she said. "Nobody will ever visit with us way down here in Louisiana where nobody ever heard of us."

My father didn't say anything except, "As long as you keep her things in there where they belong."

But right away, when there was an open house at my new school a month after we arrived, I found out my mother was prettier than the other mothers of kids in my class. Most of the mothers were fat or wore clothes that didn't fit them just right like my mother did. I watched those mothers for an hour and decided that my mother was dressed as if she expected to meet somebody, that she dressed each day with hope.

By the time of the tiny rain, we'd lived in our house for more than a year, and I was at the junior high, where boys and girls from four different grade schools came together, something I thought would make it easier, more kids to find friends among, more kids who felt like they didn't know anybody because three-fourths of them were from some other place.

It was worse. Four times as bad, and that was just among the seventh graders. There were five other grades in that school, including seniors like Bryce Daigenault and his friends, the girls with them looking more like my mother than the girls in my classes.

And right after school began there were tryouts for a football team for boys in seventh and eighth grade. My father, when he heard about the team, took me to the baseball field that was sitting empty at the end of our street and threw passes to me. "Relax your hands," he said every time I dropped the ball. "You're fighting it instead of catching it."

The football was new, a regulation one. Until then I'd been happy to chase after the half-size, soft ball my mother had given me when I started first grade. "You turn your head like that, you're going to get a face-full, and then you'll be sorry," my father said. "What are you afraid of?"

I shook my head and said, "Nothing," but he threw the ball harder, and I batted it away without even trying to catch it.

"You must get this from your mother," he said. "The closest she's ever come to relaxing is when she's asleep. She's the same now as she was when you were born. Are you?"

"What?"

"The same. You're twelve years old already. You want to grow up and be stuck with who you are right now?"

Half the boys in seventh grade tried out, but I didn't. When I was watching television instead of going to the first practice, my father took the football and poked a hole in it with a screwdriver before he dropped it in the waste basket. "We won't be needing this anymore," he said.

I walked to my grade school, six blocks away, for that first year and then to the junior-senior high that was right next to it. I didn't have to sit beside anybody on a school bus like the kids who'd gone to the other three grade schools did when they started seventh grade. Nobody knew I had a sister who'd drowned. Nobody ever ran to catch up with me as I walked, and I always made sure I didn't catch up to anyone else. It was easy.

When it rained in our yard, after my mother was on the news, there were kids who slowed down as they passed our house, but there was nothing to see. Our house was the same. And they stopped looking in a few days. It would have been better if our house had burned down and our charred and soot-covered furniture was sitting in the yard.

And then it was time for report cards and teachers starting to talk about Thanksgiving, so everyone forgot about it except Bryce, who always held out one hand, palm up, smiling like he'd never get tired of that gesture, no different than a simple wave.

On *Father Knows Best*, Bud was having problems with a girl. "Pretty soon you'll be worrying about the same thing," my mother said, but Bud looked old, like Bryce Daigenault, who drank beer on his back screened-in porch when his parents went away.

"How old is the dad?" I said.

"Robert Young? I don't know. Older than your own father, I'd bet."

"He was in a movie the day it rained in our yard."

Just then the show ended with things turning out OK like they always did. "What?" my mother said. "On television?"

Commercials came on, one of them about a car dealer in a town I knew was close to where we lived now but I'd never been to. "He was ugly in it."

"That can't be. It wasn't Robert Young then, especially if it was an old movie."

"Yes it was. He was ugly in the movie, not for real."

"Those old movies are always on. You'll see it again sometime, and you call me over to take a look. I'll come running."

"It was ancient. Pretty soon it will be something nobody will ever want to watch anymore," I said. "And anyway, Robert

Young doesn't look like anybody's father. I bet you wouldn't be married to somebody that old."

My mother put her hand on my knee the way she did when she wanted to change the subject and be serious. "Do you worry about us?" she said. "Our family?"

"No," I said, trying to stop her from talking because another show was going to start.

"What does worry you?" she said. "School? Girls?"

"I don't worry."

"You sound like your father," she said. "And he's not even around."

I was lying. But I couldn't take it back. "Worries are for women," I said, and she slapped my face.

I didn't move. I could feel how my cheek was flushed where she'd struck me, but I acted like she hadn't touched me, putting my hands in my pockets. "I know you don't mean that," she said, getting up from the couch. "I know you in your heart."

She walked up to the television and switched it off. "Maybe next week Bud will have a different problem," she said. "Maybe his little sister will die." She had her back to me. I watched her for a minute before I left the room, and I never saw her move a muscle.

The Saturday morning before Thanksgiving week I heard my father go into the room where my mother slept, and I listened for a minute to hear if he opened drawers or closets or even sat on the squeaky bed, but I didn't hear anything. It was as if I'd made a mistake, that he wasn't in there at all, and I slipped into the hall to look through the open door.

He was standing beside the card table my mother had sitting beside the bed. There wasn't any other furniture in there except for the bed and a lamp, and I could see there were photographs laid out on the table, the ones from our two hours of tiny rain, and I wondered whether he'd found them like that or he'd spread them out to examine them.

When he turned, he didn't say anything, looking back at the table and the bed as if he needed to see them again in order not to forget what was there. Right then I wondered whether he'd ever been in that room since my mother had begun to sleep there, whether he was trying to learn something from those pictures and didn't want me to know he was studying them.

"I don't know what that business was all about," he finally said. "You think you've seen everything and you haven't."

"It seems like."

"I wanted us to start over when we came all the way down here," he said. "Do you know that?"

"Yes," I said, although I thought, at that moment, that he meant just himself.

"Things change, and you think they're different but they're not," he said. "Does that make sense?"

"Yes," I said, meaning it this time, and he nodded like he'd expected me to agree all along.

He opened the closet, and I saw that every item was one of Eileen's Gym-Starz outfits. All of Eileen's regular clothes were gone. He ran his hand along the length of them until he touched the last outfit on the right. "Here's what I bought for her for the day she joined Andromeda. Just one size bigger because she was so good I knew she was going to move right up."

When I didn't say anything, he stared at me. "Andromeda,"

he said. "You know what that is—the girls' traveling team, the one that has their scores kept and goes to other towns all over Ohio?"

"Yes."

"You know all about it? You ever look that up in a book to know what that constellation looks like? You ever look up in the sky and see that beautiful girl made of stars?"

I started to leave, but he grabbed my arm and held it so tightly I winced. "What's in your closet, Brad?" he said. "Toys?" For a moment I was sure he was going to drag me into my room to look, but he let go, closed the closet, and disappeared down the hall.

Eileen hit her head is what the doctor said. She was likely unconscious when she went into the water. She could do back flips and she could swim. And that day while I followed my mother as far as the kitchen door, watching her talk on the phone for what she said later was "a minute, maybe two," Eileen had probably tossed herself backward off the edge of the pool and slipped as she pushed off, tumbling backwards so awkwardly that her head hit the side of the pool.

"Bradley was right there where I could see him," she told my father, "so I thought Eileen was right nearby because she'd been told."

My father had glared at both of us—my mother for being negligent and me for being obedient. I was so afraid of everything that I always obeyed. I knew exactly what he thought. If I'd run off like Eileen, I would have seen her fall, and she'd still be alive.

The day after Thanksgiving was warm, and Bryce had a friend over who was throwing a football around with him in his backyard. After a while Bryce signaled him to run farther for each pass until he ran halfway into our yard, the long spiral landing softly on his outstretched hands but tumbling off and bouncing against the house. "Good hands," Bryce shouted, and the other boy, as he picked up the ball, sneered at me as if I'd laughed out loud.

"You think you could catch it, twerp?" he said.

"Maybe."

"No chance in hell," he said, and I watched as he took a few steps closer to Bryce as if he was distracted rather than shortening the distance because he couldn't throw the ball that far. When he finally let it go, the ball wobbled and nosed into the ground at Bryce's feet. "Johnny Unitas," Bryce said. "Have another beer."

When I heard somebody laugh, I saw there was a girl sitting on the Daigenaults' screened-in porch. The boy who'd dropped the ball looked back at me and said, "You think it's funny, you little pussy? Huh?" I didn't say anything, but I wished I had because there was no way that boy could come back and beat me up, not a twelve-year-old in front of Bryce and that girl.

And when my mother stepped onto the porch a moment later, I thought she might have been listening by the window, trying to learn what my life was like by overhearing a part of it at a time. "Your father's leaving," she said. "Go outside and tell him goodbye."

For years she had told me to give him a hug when he was about to leave, but that afternoon she didn't, and maybe because she said something different, I didn't get up at first. Just for a few seconds, but my mother noticed because she said, "He's your father," before she turned back into the house.

My father was already out front beside the car. His suitcase was on the front seat, and he was closing the passenger-side door. "I'm off," he said. "Back to the old grind."

"See ya," I said, but I stayed by the door, holding it open with one hand in a way that I thought would make him say, "You'll let the flies in."

He had a tie looped around his neck, but it wasn't knotted, and his shirt was still open at the collar. He glanced down and held both ends of the tie with his hands as if he'd just remembered to knot it, but then he let go and walked around the car, opened the door, and got in without speaking again.

That night, after I watched television for two hours straight without my mother telling me to shut it off, I went outside at ten o'clock when the news came on, taking a beer out of the refrigerator and replacing it with one from my father's case in the pantry. I walked down to the baseball field, sipping the beer, but it tasted awful, and by the time I got to the field, I poured half of what was left on the ground by home plate, so what I was carrying was nearly empty, and I could imagine feeling different.

I cut through all the backyards on our side of the street to get home, dumping the rest of the beer on the Daigenaults' lawn and tossing the can into the trees that bordered their yard. The can snagged on some branches, scraping against them before falling, and when I heard a sound from the Daigenaults' porch, I thought I'd been seen, that somebody was about to stride across the lawn to run me into the woods to retrieve that can.

I ducked down, but nobody stepped off the porch. I heard a girl's voice, soft, nearly purring, and I crept closer, making out Bryce and a girl from the high school in the dim light that seeped through the Daigenaults' blinds. "We see you out there," Bryce said. "You can stop acting like it's hide-and-seek."

I stood up. The girl and Bryce both had their shirts off. There were beer bottles on a table. The girl was fat in her stomach, and her breasts, without a bra to hold them up, sagged like she was older than my mother.

"It's rain boy," Bryce said. "You want a beer?"

The girl laughed. "You getting a good look?" she said. "You a little peeper?"

"You should have waited a few more minutes," Bryce said. "You would have seen everything."

The girl didn't laugh this time. She hooked her bra on and buttoned her blouse. "You're a real shit," she said to Bryce. "You and your skinny pervert neighbor."

Bryce winked at me and took a long swallow of beer before he turned and followed the girl into the house. "Hey now, baby," he was saying. "Hey now, baby." He didn't close the door, but I thought if I took even one more step closer Bryce would come back out with a gun and shoot me, still smiling like we were friends.

When I turned I stepped into the flower bed Mrs. Daigenault had planted the length of the house in the back. Three of the flowers were bent under my shoe. Even though it was November, they'd been in bloom for two weeks and were fading, but for a moment I stared at the broken stems before I started to run, slipping, and catching myself just late enough with my hands that I knew there would be a grass stain on my right knee.

Inside the house, I rubbed at that stain for a second before giving up, and I thought of all the stories I could tell somebody like Bryce if I didn't run away like a baby. My life was full of them, and not only the small rain. My sister's dying in our back-yard swimming pool while my mother answered the phone that rang just as she unlocked the gate to the fence that surrounded it. "You stay right there," she said, and Eileen did, while I followed her inside and listened to her talk while Eileen drowned.

"Who were you gabbing with that was so important?" my father asked the day after the accident.

"Grace Yerger," my mother said. "She called me."

"And you had to run back in and answer like it might be the president calling from the White House."

"The phone rings and you stop what you're doing to answer," she said. "That's the way it works, Bob. How else is there to find out who's calling and what they might need?"

"Grace Yerger calls every day, and it's always about church and some do-gooding she's up to."

"Not every day."

"You two yakking it up so you didn't even hear Eileen splash. If it had been Jesus his own self, I wish to fuck you'd have let it ring."

"You don't mean that," she said, and my father stared at her, taking one deep breath before he said, "I'd rather be in hell than have my daughter dead."

When I walked into the living room, my mother was sitting in the chair that faced the backyard. "I was just watching the news, and when I shut it off I sat here to think for a while."

"What about?"

"I hate the South," she said. "Here it is almost December and as warm as April. It makes your thoughts get crooked. The trees and such never get a chance to rest." She looked at me. "Bradley, does it seem like that to you? Keep you up at night?"

"No," I said.

"Because you're young, likely as not. You might turn out to be southern, and I wouldn't care for that."

"I lived ten years in Cleveland," I said. "That's long enough to remember winter forever."

"That's good," she said. "Weather's important to who you are. I was thinking it won't ever snow like it rained for us. Not here in this yard. If we get that special weather, it will be just like before."

I didn't know what to say next. I sat with my back to the window and waited for her to go on. "Your father is such a realist," she finally said. "He doesn't imagine the world is anything but what he sees."

I wanted to talk, but I had to swallow the way I did when we had to sing by ourselves in front of the class for a music test at school. "Are you listening to me?" she said, and I heard myself say "Yes" in a voice so high I sounded like a girl.

"Your father thinks I don't know what he does because I'm not there to see." I waited, listening to the way air whistled when she breathed through her nose, thinking maybe there were words in there. "He travels a lot," she said. "Are you following me?"

"Yes," I said, my voice back down to boy-sounding.

"So you know?"

"Yes." My mother didn't speak then, and her breath was like mine, quiet because she'd opened her mouth and let the air come silently to her.

"Your father has a friend in town," my mother said. "You understand what I mean by a friend?"

"Yes."

"Do you now? Just like that?"

I nodded because I did, just like that knowing my father had a woman like Bryce Daigenault had that girl on his porch, that right that minute he might be with her in another room believing he was happy.

I sat up straight and waited, but after a while I knew she was looking out the window rather than looking at me. I didn't move or turn my head. There, in the dark, I knew she'd tell me if something happened outside.

After a while, when she didn't say anything else, I thought my mother, sitting like she did with her legs resting across a soft, cloth-covered stool, would fall asleep in her chair. I didn't want to be awake and see her asleep like that, someone for whom it didn't matter where she slept. But for a few more moments I sat there and decided she was thinking, right then, about the rest of her life and whether living in that house with my father was something she could manage for even a few more weeks.

She should have told me to leave the room, but maybe she wanted me there because I reminded her of the miracle we'd shared. It rained only on us for two hours, and everyone knew the rain was real and not made up like spacemen and Bigfoot and the Loch Ness Monster. I could stand exactly like my mother had when I first saw her in the rain. I could lift my head up and keep my eyes open and remember how her blouse stuck to her body and showed how beautiful she still was, as if that rain had chosen her to fall on.

And what I wanted to tell her was how terrible it was that my father was always going to come back.

THE WORST THING

You DON'T EXPECT TO KNOW murderers when their stories make the newspapers. Not if you're normal. Not if you own a house surrounded by other well-kept houses.

But there she was on the front page, Amy Bender, a face I recognized, and she'd killed her own baby, one just a minute old. Given birth in her bathtub and let her newborn daughter drown. Told her boyfriend to take the body outside and throw it in the garbage, making sure it was good and covered by whatever else was in the can.

It's hard to read these things. I know I stopped a few times that first day of her news and sipped coffee. I ate a third chocolate-iced, custard-filled doughnut, what I haven't done for ten years or more. And there I was just retired, two weeks into the first summer that wouldn't end the last Monday in August when school took up again.

Those fourth graders would get along without me. The school had hired a woman who was younger than all three of my daughters, and though her age didn't bother me, it bothered me that I'd been the only male teacher at Governor Snyder Elementary School, and now there it was all women again, kindergarten through fourth grade at the school named after the one Pennsylvania governor who'd ever come from our county. Like the old days, like the fifties, when I reached seventh grade, before I ever met a man in school.

* * *

"You won't even know you've retired until September," my wife kept saying, but Connie was wrong. I felt like I'd died, like I'd been buried and the dirt piled on. "You just need something to keep you busy," Connie said, and there was some truth to that.

She'd been a teacher too, thirty years and out four years ago even with the three girls of her own to tend along the way, somebody content with weight-control swimming classes, book club meetings, and three days a week of volunteer work. She'd taught Spanish at the high school in the same district where I'd taught, and she'd counted down the last fifty days on a big sheet of paper she stuck to the refrigerator with magnets. "It's different there," she'd said of the high school. "Not as hopeful. Even the good kids are hard now."

For years people had remarked that the two of us were inside-out: Connie at the high school like a man, me with the young like a woman. And then, these past ten years, that sort of thinking slowed down and nearly stopped, muted like all the opinions about gender and race and ethnicity that people learned to at least keep to themselves.

But that baby-killing woman, that Amy Bender, she'd had a boy in my class last year and a girl the year before. I remembered those two children, both of them terrible students, the kind you know won't finish high school, the girl likely to be pregnant by sixteen, maybe sooner. You're not supposed to think that way about nine- and ten-year-olds, but there's no denying experience.

Right then, as I read about their mother while I crammed that extra doughnut down my throat, I wondered where those children, just ten and eleven years old, had been when all this was going on. And that article, as if the writer understood what any reader would want to know, answered that question on page two: Louisiana. I'd thought the boy had just followed his sister to the middle school, but in fact his father had taken him. The girl, too, though the whereabouts of her own father remained unknown.

"There's something that calls for the word *piacular*," I said to Connie.

She made the face she uses every time I mention one of the weird, rare words I'd started studying during the last three days of school when there was nothing left to do but collect books, fill in report cards, and show a movie approved by the principal before following my class outside, rare-word dictionary in hand, for the races the school called "Field Day Olympics." "OK," she said now, "get it over with."

"It's an adjective that means 'requiring atonement.'"

"Piacular," she said. "No wonder nobody ever uses that word. It doesn't mean anything to anybody."

"You've been telling me for years to get a hobby," I said.

"It's not a hobby," she said. "It's just you reading that one stupid book you bought when we were in Harrisburg for Memorial Day."

"Reading's a hobby."

"No, it's not. It's just what anybody does who has a brain. Book club is a hobby."

She gathered up the box the doughnuts had come in as if she needed to get the last two away from me. "Aboulia," I said. "Have you ever heard that word spoken?"

"Of course not."

"It means 'loss of will,'" I said. "It's a perfectly good word. It's not the word's fault nobody knows it."

"Yes, it is," Connie said at once. "If the word was any good, people would use it." She moved my place mat and squirted Windex on the glass-topped kitchen table, beginning to wipe it down.

"Sometimes they get used. There are weird words in that book I bought that I've actually heard of."

"Name one," she said, not moving to her side of the table, which looked spotless though she'd eaten one glazed doughnut herself.

"*Karoshi*. It's Japanese."

"I don't speak Japanese."

"It means that you die from overwork. You wear yourself right out."

"Those Japanese must have a lot of teachers," Connie said, "but you don't need for them to give you a word for what you already know. You're like somebody who watches reality shows and knows the names of the people who get thrown out in the first few weeks."

"Bloviate," I said. "I read that word in the newspaper just this year."

Connie replaced the Windex in the cupboard above the stove, and for a moment I thought she was going to give in. "Not our newspaper," she said at last. "That's a big city newspaper word."

During July I went once to Connie's swimming class and twice to her book club. If I had been alone, I would have left swimming after five minutes when I found out what we were doing, something like treading water, only easier because we had little inner tubes to keep us up so we could walk in the water as slowly as a bride coming toward the altar. Worse than that, the bodies of all the men were horrible, like premonitions I didn't need to see.

"You can't quit everything after one try," Connie said, and I agreed, choosing to go back to book club because it was twice a month instead of twice a week, so I had time to convince myself it wasn't as boring as I'd thought it was listening to women talk like Oprah, acting like saying "I was so moved" meant the writer had accomplished something special.

When I returned, though, the library where the meeting was held served refreshments, and I was stuck holding a cup of green tea and watching women eat honey-bran muffins dusted with sprinkles colored red, white, and blue for the upcoming holiday. The woman who led the discussions sat so straight that two crumbs from the cake on her fork fell across the swelling of her breasts and lay there, balanced, while she ate as if she were being tested and points might be deducted for bending over the table or allowing her left arm to leave her side. It was only when she lifted her napkin to her lips after three bites that she noticed the crumbs, brushing them into her napkin, then taking a new one to press to her lips after two more bites.

"You get your own things to do then," Connie said when I vowed never to go back. "Don't ruin it for me."

The drowned baby case reappeared in the newspaper the following week. A trial date had been set for the beginning of October because Amy Bender, after confessing in detail, had retracted her statement and intended to plead not guilty. "They'll say she's insane," Connie said.

"It says in the paper that the boyfriend is sticking by his story."

"The guy she told to throw the baby in the garbage?" She tore her doughnut in half and put the uneaten part back in the box.

"He'll testify. He'll say she knew what she was doing."

The boyfriend had kept the body instead of dumping it. He'd tried to bury it. "Like the proper way," he'd said, though that turned out to be inside a plastic bag and under a pile of leaves when he couldn't make a hole in the ground deep enough with his hands. According to the newspaper, he was mentally challenged.

"Retarded," Connie said. "Why don't they let reporters use real words? They almost sound as bad as those things you come up with from reading that book of yours."

"Leighster," I said, and though Connie shook her head in a way that said, "Stop it," I went on. "That's the word for 'female liar.' See? We need that word to get this situation just right."

"Is there a word in that book for a man who lies?"

"Not so far."

"There won't be. Think *bitch*."

"This isn't about politics."

"A liar's a liar then. Female's got nothing to do with it."

It seemed to me that it did, but until I found an archaic or rare word for a male liar, I had to let it go. "It sure sounds like that boyfriend's retarded," I said, moving on as best as I could.

"It makes you wonder when you walk in the woods," Connie said. "There's no telling what's there. That could have been you finding that child with all the walking you do. You should be keeping an eye out."

"There can't be another dead baby so soon in the same town. It's crazy to think that way."

"No, it's not." Connie looked out the window as if she were thinking about going for a walk. "So what do you think?" she said. "Isn't this the worst thing possible?"

"There's always worse," I said, though right then nothing came to me.

"The pessimist," she said. "Like you can come up with something awful nobody's even thought of yet."

"Somebody will do it for me. All it needs is a name."

Connie turned toward me again. "Get something besides doughnuts when you go for your walk," she said. "Get something healthy for once."

When she got up and left the kitchen without wiping the table, I finished her half-eaten glazed. Doughnuts don't keep, let alone one broken in half.

* * *

The last time I'd seen Amy Bender in the flesh was at the school spring open house the year before. She'd shown up right at 9:00 p.m., the time everything ended. The last of my students' parents was leaving as she came through the door. Some of the other rooms were already dark, the teachers gone. "It's some job you have, isn't it?" she said, staying near the door where the students' "Skeleton Stories" were posted on a bulletin board.

"Do you have questions about your son's progress?" I said. She bent down and peered at the stories. "Roy's doing fine," I added.

When she straightened, I thought she was going to approach my desk, but she stayed beside the door. "You don't have to lie to me," she said. "My kid's dumb as a stump. He gets it from his dad."

The light went off in the room across the hall. She turned to watch Mary Cressinger close her door and disappear down the hall, and then she took two steps to the side and checked the bulletin board again. When she bent down to see the lowest row of stories, her skirt rode up her thick thighs.

"Here it is," she said. "Roy's masterpiece."

I knew what she was seeing. Her son's story was three sentences long, all of them beginning with "skeltens are . . ."

". . . skery as a monster."

". . . skiny as a witch."

". . . spooky as a ghost."

"He got one right," Amy Bender said, but she didn't say whether it was spelling or semantic accuracy she was talking about. All of the adjectives and nouns her son had used had been listed on the blackboard before the children wrote. The next shortest story had six sentences. A small skeleton, skinny as an icicle, had walked into school and eaten so much pizza in the cafeteria that it had turned into a fat boy.

"Where do they get all these ideas from?" she said. "Do you tell them stories?"

"We read."

She stared at Roy's story a second time. "Will he be bringing this home before too long?"

"It's his to keep after they all come down next week."

"Good," she said, and finally she stood up straight and looked directly at me. "Roy's happy here, right?" she said. "He don't act sad?" When I nodded, she didn't say anything else.

* * *

Connie was right to tell me to cut down on the doughnuts. I'd started walking for the exercise but always ended up stopping at the grocery store, just over a mile from our house. Going that direction meant I had to pass the school where I'd taught, and for over a month I'd made a right angle turn on the sidewalk, not saving even one step by cutting on a diagonal across its parking lot. But one morning in August, when the playground was empty, I veered up the grassy slope and slipped through the gate in the fence that ran a few feet above the street. Nostalgia, I thought, a way to look in the back windows where my room had been located while I saved a bit of time and energy.

That was my intention until, just before I reached the fence on the opposite side, I noticed a condom beside the sliding board. A used one, stretched and limp. Something that must have been dropped there the night before because surely the custodian or a mother bringing her small child to the playground would dispose of it immediately.

I looked at the sliding board and tried to picture the couple. I lay on the slide to feel what it would be like to be the girl on her back as she draped her legs over the sides. The boy, I thought, would have had to have pushed her up the slide because it seemed impossible to reach her if she were lying near the bottom.

From where I lay I was facing the rear of the school. A janitor worked nights during the school year, but his shift changed to daylight in the summer. He could have been watching me right then. Maybe he checked from time to time as a sentry against men who might be loitering to watch children play.

I sat up, bent over, and lifted the condom carefully between the tips of my thumb and little finger, the small weight of it reminding me of how my mother had always made me spit my chewed gum into a tissue and wrap it before I could throw it away.

I looked under the seesaws and the swings before I carried the condom to the trash barrel by the gate, but the ground beneath them was bare. I peered into the trash barrel, but all I could see were soda cans and the empty bags that had held potato chips and pretzels. I dropped the condom, and it looked so terrible draped across a soda can that I reached down and stirred the cans until it was covered. I had to fling two ants off my fingers when I was finished.

For the next three nights I rented movies to watch with Connie, timing them so they ended late enough that we went directly to bed. It was all I could do not to tell her I was going for a walk at eleven o'clock. And though I passed the playground earlier each day, it was another week before the yard was empty when I approached it. I walked past every piece of playground equipment, but there was nothing but ordinary trash on the ground near any of it.

By the time September began, with both of us home in the middle of the morning, we sought out different rooms. I read for an hour. Then I just sat there with my feet up, thinking about watching television, but embarrassed to turn it on at 10:30. Because she didn't read except in bed, I had no idea what Connie could be doing, and when I finally came out of the spare room at eleven o'clock, she was putting on her jacket. "It's my day at the day-care center," she said. "I'm having lunch with Ellen Foster before we sign in for our five hours."

"I'm having lunch by myself," I said, "before I go crazy."

"We've never lived together like this," Connie said. "It's different."

"We've always only had summers together, three months at a time."

"Those were vacations," she said. "This is our regular life."

"You mean you can't stand having me around all day."

"Not exactly."

"I bet there's a word for that version of 'not exactly.' I bet married people invented it while they waited out their last days together."

"Maybe you could substitute," she said. "Work off some of that energy."

"Maybe not."

Connie frowned. I could have told her I'd already thought of that and decided it was impossible, that the classroom had to be mine or I didn't want to be there. It was like having children. I could love my own three daughters, but I could never adopt. It sounded like selfishness, something to never say.

A week later, when I shuffled out of the spare room at 10:15, she told me to get in the car. She drove for ten minutes and pulled off the road in front of a house so new the yard around it was bare earth. There was even a wooden plank to walk on in order to reach the front door. "Come inside," she said, producing a key. "Take a look."

The house was small—two bedrooms, one bathroom—like the one I'd grown up in with my older brother. "What do you want me to see?" I said.

"This is a Habitat house. We were going to start painting the inside this weekend, but the construction foreman said to give him a few more days."

"You want me to help when you're ready?"

"It would do you good."

"How many are there of you?"

"It varies," she said, and I knew that meant the number was small. "This isn't book club. We're doing something here."

"I think I'll go to the trial," I said. "The baby killer's. It starts in a week."

As if she were getting ready to paint, Connie nudged a leftover sheet of wall board into the center of the room where we were standing. "I hope it lasts as long as O.J.'s."

"That's not likely," I said.

"Neither was his. It was open and shut, and look what happened."

"I want it complicated. I want it to be like school. You'll be happy to know I put in my name for substituting."

"Good," Connie said.

"They'll probably not even call me," I said. "They had three young women last year who substituted, and all of them applied for my job. One of them got hired, so the other ones will try to keep their hands in."

"Those other two have moved on," Connie said. "That's how it happens. But don't expect to be called right off the bat. You know that teachers never miss school the first few weeks. You just have to wait until reality sets in on them."

"I'm counting on it. That trial is right around the corner."

"Maybe not. It will take a while to choose a jury for something like this," Connie said. "You might be teaching again before they find twelve people around here who haven't already decided they'd like to drown that woman themselves."

***

It took three days to pick the jury. I stayed home after the first half day of listening to routine questions that eliminated dozens of people who said, flat-out, they'd made up their minds or they would always believe the word of a police officer more than that of someone who wasn't.

For a minute, outside the court house, I stood among a small group of men who'd been dismissed, all four of them stopping to light cigarettes. "That bitch gave herself a Polish abortion," I heard somebody say, like the death of that child could be an ethnic joke.

There was a parking ticket under the windshield wiper of my car. Ten dollars, it asked for. "Pay within forty-eight hours or be subject to an additional fine." I looked at my watch and saw it was nine minutes over the two hours the meter allowed. I noticed no one in uniform on either side of the street. It must have taken a few minutes to record my license plate number.

I subtracted until I decided there was an asshole on the job, somebody who started writing up the ticket while the last minute or two counted down on the digital timer. But when those smokers walked past me still laughing, I thought I deserved to be fined for saying nothing about cruelty.

* * *

By the time they'd chosen a jury, it was Friday. Monday was Columbus Day, something I realized only because court was closed. I walked to the grocery store, and for a moment I was surprised that the school parking lot was full of cars, and yet mothers with small children were in the playground. In-service day, I remembered. A way, besides relaxation, for teachers to use a holiday.

At the grocery, a mother of one of my final-year students stopped me by the bakery. The boy I'd had acted shy when he saw me, like the fathers of the children I'd taught, rural men who came to conferences wearing ball caps and bowling jackets. She had three more children with her. "Eight, six, and seven months now for the little girl," she said.

"You have your hands full," I said, and she didn't smile when she answered, "That's for sure."

"I wanted all my boys to have you," she said. "Their father flew the coop after I started showing with the baby, and they could all use a man." I watched, alarmed, as the baby squirmed in her arms, arching her back so violently that she seemed likely to tumble to the floor.

"I didn't expect the little one would see you at the blackboard," she said. "Last time we met I was big as a house, but I thought you had enough juice left for the boys."

"Forty years," I said. "A nice round number."

She looked puzzled, and then she pulled at the baby, repositioning her. The boys had disappeared into another aisle— magazines, I thought, candy. "Well," she said, "we all make do, don't we?"

"Most."

"Is that so?" she said. "I didn't know there was another choice." The baby was chewing on her collar. One of the boys, the youngest, reappeared carrying a cheap plastic toy. "Put that back," she said, and when he answered, "Want this," I pushed my cart toward the case where six varieties of muffins were displayed. When I passed him, he slapped at the cart. "Want this," he said again as if I might pay for it. When I turned into the next aisle, not stopping, the baby began to cry.

***

You'd think you would have heard everything nearing sixty-five with forty years of teaching inside you, but I sat there in the courtroom on Tuesday and heard the coroner testify that Amy Bender had stuffed toilet paper down the baby's throat. A wad of it. Blue. To make sure that baby would die and not somehow breathe in water like it had gills.

The defense lawyer didn't cross-examine, but there was a murmur in that courtroom. And I knew I'd made a sound in my throat and let it loose. Something between a moan and a cough. It didn't sound like anything I'd ever uttered, but the judge looked right at me sitting by myself off to the side like I was, nobody near me.

Which was something else I wondered about—why hardly anybody had come to watch and listen. Now that the crowd of prospective jurors had disappeared, it was like a funeral with just the preacher and family. As if the dead had no friends. As if maybe those few were there by obligation, seeing to it that things didn't fall apart, the dead just discarded like there was a plague or a war.

The next day two policemen testified, but after the business about the blue toilet paper, their stories sounded so tame I thought the prosecutor had handled things wrong, that he'd given up the punch line before telling his awful joke. By the third day, when a psychologist claimed that Amy Bender was sane and then spent a few hours being questioned by the defense lawyer, anyone could tell the district attorney was sprinting toward a verdict.

On the fourth, and as it turned out, the last day of testimony, there were exactly twelve spectators in the courtroom, as if we formed another jury. I was younger than most of them, and I wondered if the older ones attended trials as a hobby, whether they sat through DUI hearings and divorce proceedings the way some people sit through television.

Someone here, I thought, must be related to Amy Bender, but there was no telling who. The three men were older than I was. Two women were of an age that could make them her mother, but neither of them sat alone.

In the morning, the boyfriend testified. He spoke like a child. "I was scared," he said. "I knew Amy had hurt the baby bad." He looked straight at the lawyer as if he was being photographed for a driver's license. "I gave it a nice place. I said a prayer for it."

"What did you say?" the district attorney prompted.

"A prayer. You know. Now I lay me down to sleep. That one."

"Thank you."

The defense lawyer made it seem as if that boy wasn't so dumb he might have planned the murder, as if he might have thought to pray when he realized what he had done. This is what it is to be court-appointed, I thought. Seeing to it that Amy Bender wasn't just thrown into the river inside a sack full of stones while an audience applauded.

* * *

Amy Bender testified right after lunch, the only defense witness. "The baby was born dead," she said. "I panicked." When the public defender asked why she had said otherwise when arrested, she answered, "I was so afraid I got confused."

There was a moment before the district attorney rose from his chair to cross-examine, and I spent it looking at Amy Bender, who had the first signs of gray beginning just above her ears where her hair was cut nearly as short as a man's, even the longest part of it barely reaching the collar of the jacket of her tan pants suit. The gray-haired mother—the phrase sounded like the beginning of an essay about the weary and impoverished. It was more than hair color—she was soft in a way that made her shapeless. She had a belly on her, and I thought it was possible she was pregnant again. This woman looked like a grandmother, and yet she was thirty-three years old.

Had she shown gray eighteen months ago? I wasn't sure, just as I didn't remember how fat she'd been in the belly. And now she wore a pant suit that looked new but out of style. It made me think of a woman I worked with who'd worn pant suits every day, a wardrobe of them, as if she'd settled on a fashion so comfortable that she didn't notice when other women left them in closets and finally in boxes beside the Goodwill bin. It made me think she wanted to cover every part of her body.

Connie was paint-spattered when she walked into the house at five o'clock. Habitat, I thought, and saw that she'd painted in one of the shirts I'd still worn for teaching last spring. "I thought you just worked on weekends," I said.

"Old people can paint on Wednesday," she said. "It's like jury duty. Haven't you noticed?"

I hadn't. I couldn't remember the face or age of any juror. "What?" I said. "You think everybody on the jury is retired?"

"Old people decide who's guilty and who's not. We're justice."

"You declared her guilty before the trial started."

"That's why we're needed," Connie said. "So at least some people get what they deserve."

***

I didn't go back for the verdict the next Monday morning because the phone rang at 6:45, and by 8:30 I was a teacher again, welcoming third graders into the room beside the one I'd taught in. The eight-year-old boy I'd seen in the grocery store sat in the third row. "Caleb's brother, right?" I said, and the boy looked around at his classmates to see if they'd noticed.

"Yes," he said.

A girl raised her hand. "You're Mr. Steinmetz," she said. "My brother had you, too."

To my relief, they settled down to reading and stayed quiet through social studies and spelling. At lunch the radio in the teacher's lounge announced that Amy Bender had been found guilty. "The jury was out less than an hour," the newscaster said.

By afternoon the class was restless, and so was I. I looked out the window and saw the playground. A woman had strapped her small child into what my students, despite my reprimands, had always called "the retard swing," and she was pushing it in small arcs. There was another hour, and all that was left was a lesson in fractions. Half the class was whispering to each other in pairs. "Hold on a minute," I said. "What do you call it when you say you're sorry for something wrong that you did?"

Three voices chorused, "Apology."

"What do you call it when you're so angry at the person who apologized that all you can think of is 'You should be sorry?'"

"Mad," a girl said, and I shook my head.

"Pissed off," a boy called out, and the room hushed, waiting to see what I would do.

I shook my head again, but they were stumped. "Antapology," I said, and I printed it on the board.

"Cool," said the boy who'd offered "pissed off," but I could see that most of the class was already drifting.

"I want to tell you a story about the worst thing that ever happened," I said, and they sat up like the jury had when Amy Bender had testified.

"It's a short story," I said. "A baby is born. A little boy. But his mother is a witch, and he is so beautiful she never feeds him, and pretty soon he's so skinny he's almost dead."

"That sounds like Snow White," the girl whose brother had been in my class said, "only with a boy."

"But if she doesn't feed him, he won't get to grow up, so he won't even have a name."

The girl frowned and glanced around the room as if she expected somebody to take her side. "No witch is that mean," she said. "She'd at least wait until she found out if she had a good reason to hate him."

"That's what makes it the worst," I said. "She doesn't want to wait."

I walked down the aisle, brushing the tops of their heads with my hands as I spoke. "She doesn't want to wait until he's in school. She doesn't want to wait until he can talk and tell stories, too."

The last two rows bowed their heads as I approached. I'd never had such silence in a classroom. It seemed a miracle that they had lived. "There's a word for that," I said. "Ugsome,"

"That's not a word," the girl said, but she looked around the room to see if anyone had heard it before.

"Yes, it is. I found it in a book. It means 'really horrible.'"

"Like when you say 'ugh' when somebody pukes?" Caleb's brother said.

"Worse than that," I said, and then I stopped. For a minute, I'd been eager to speak, but now all of my forty years of teaching checked my tongue. Now that I was back in the classroom, I wanted to be called again.

They watched as I spelled *ugsome* on the board. "Sometimes there's only one time for a word to be used," I said, and they all stared at the blackboard. "Once you use it, you'll never hear it again."

Nobody spoke. "Now," I said, "I want you to write the end to that story I told you. Make it turn out the way you want it to."

A girl began to cry. "What if it's too late to save the baby?"

I looked at the blackboard before I answered. "Here's one thing I didn't tell you," I said. "Even though he was so skinny, that boy was still beautiful."

The girl smiled. Then they all began to work. Twenty-six third graders concentrated, their heads down and pencils moving.

ISN'T SHE SOMETHING?

"I'M WITH SOMEONE NEW," LARRY Whisenant's daughter said. "Lanie."

"As in Elaine?" he asked.

"Lanie," Amanda said, "as in Lanie. She's transgendered."

Whisenant tried to give her a reporter's reaction, but it came out as, "That must be different," and when Amanda glared at him, he added, "I didn't mean that as a judgment."

"At least not without seeing her first?"

"Yes," he said.

"Lanie's birth name is Lawrence," she said. "She's nearly finished with her preoperative period."

Whisenant couldn't form another sentence. He understood that his daughter was sleeping with a man who was very soon going to have a sex-change operation, that what she could plainly see as a sign of how aroused he was would disappear, folded inside him like a handkerchief in a pocket. He felt a numbness behind his eyes, something he was sure would drift into a headache he thought of at once as the very first one he'd ever had brought on by sexual ambivalence.

Over the years, he'd developed an immune system for what columnists in the newspapers where his work appeared coyly called "alternative lifestyles." His daughter, now twenty-four, had come out at sixteen. Though recently she'd tested him again when she'd nearly shaved her head, leaving her hair bristly and short, even for the Marines. Stubble. Like the beginning of a beard on her skull. It looked like Sluggo's. When he'd used that name with Amanda a week earlier, she'd said, "Who's that?" and he hadn't bothered to tell her.

He'd imagined her opting for boots and camouflage, but she still wore jeans like half the young women he could see in the university student lounge. Her tank top was tight in a way that turned the heads of young men. Sexy, he thought, in spite of himself, her shoulders bare in a way that always took his eyes toward a woman, the straps running down to where her breasts pulled the material forward enough he could see a flash of dark bra cup.

He searched the lounge for another woman with hair as short, but only two had cropped hair, and each of them wore it styled in a tight, ambiguous wave.

"I'm reading your articles on Bringiton.com," Amanda said, generously changing the subject.

Whisenant had spent a month as a security guard at a high school, and the story had been carried four consecutive weeks in the Sunday magazine of the *Philadelphia Inquirer*, but his daughter hadn't read a newspaper since she'd been required to by her senior social studies teacher in high school. Whisenant had never heard of Bringiton.com, and that, for certain, meant they hadn't paid to reproduce his series of articles. He thought of calling the newspaper and telling them to have it taken down. "Do you have a subscription to this Bringiton?" he asked.

"It's a free site, Dad. They put up things that shake people up. Muckraking—right?"

"Sometimes."

"What I want to know is how did you keep from getting depressed?" she said. "That job sounded even worse than your month of washing dishes in that Chinese restaurant."

"It's the teachers who get depressed," he said. "I was doing maintenance, making sure the weeds didn't get too thick."

She frowned. He was lying like he always did when he talked, diminishing things. In the articles, he'd written about specific, troubled students he'd come to know and the ways in which he'd tried to reach them. Nobody, not even the school administrators, had known he had taken the job for research. It was the only way he'd recognize how the guards were treated by teachers and administrators.

"I shouldn't even be asking," she said. "Forget it." They'd had this conversation about his immersion journalism a dozen times, so he was happy to let it pass, her complaining to him about his stupid persona of indifference, an argument that had ended, once, during her last summer at home before college, with his describing in detail the elaborate ways in which she created herself as a lesbian before she walked out the door.

"I'm in the middle of a new project," he said. "It's a doozy."

"Doozy? You sound like Grandma."

"It's all I can say right now. But doozy covers it nicely."

What he was keeping from his daughter, at least for now, was that, for his next series of articles, he had a part in a movie. This time he was enjoying himself, writing about being a zombie in a horror film. What it felt like to be made up and lurch along. Already he knew that only four of the actors who had speaking parts had any chance of escaping at the end. All the other beautiful girls and boys were going to be torn apart and eaten because it didn't matter if he and the other zombies got shot a hundred times. They'd look uglier, of course, more problems with their complexions and how well they could walk, but they were relentless. There was even a chance this movie would allow them to be zombies forever because so far it looked as if there were always going to be resurrections, the last few pages of the script a secret so everybody, according to the director, stayed on their toes, even the actors who were slaughtered halfway through the film.

"Next time we talk," Whisenant told his daughter, "I'll tell you about it. You know how it is. I don't have anything to say about something until I do it."

***

For Whisenant, the worst moment of every day was when he returned home and entered to silence. Someone loved was expected—the phrase had risen in him one late afternoon more than a year ago, and by now it was as constant as the latch clicking back into place when he closed the door.

It had been two and a half years since his wife had died after being struck by a van while walking the dog. The distraught driver had been the only witness. "The dog lunged at road kill or something, and she was half spun around and stumbled two steps into the road. You know how it would be with the leash and all. That big-ass dog just yanked her right into the road. What's a woman doing walking a dog that size?"

The answer was Whisenant had been out of town getting material by working in the nuclear power station at Three Mile

Island. He'd come home every other night, but the trip, ninety miles each way, was one he didn't want to make every day, and Marie had been walking his Newfoundland for nearly four weeks without a problem. In fact, she'd walked that dog for weeks at a time for the three years they'd owned it, his present to himself when his daughter had gone off to college. After the accident, however, even though the dog survived with injuries that weren't permanent, Whisenant had had the Newfoundland put down.

But even now, he found its black hairs attached to his clothes. It made the dog more of a presence, somehow, than his wife, although he hadn't touched a thing of hers since the accident. The medicine chest was still stocked with sun block and body lotion and three kinds of pain relievers he'd never tried, sticking to aspirin. Now, with the news of his daughter's transgendered lover throbbing beneath his skull, he stepped into the shower, and Marie's shampoo and conditioner were still in the basket that hung from the nozzle. Whisenant stood under the hot water for fifteen minutes. Even though all of his makeup had been cleaned off before he'd left the set, his skin itched. Altogether, he'd been a zombie for just two hours, long enough to be photographed alone and among the other zombies to evaluate the fright level of the special effects before they were put into action. Tomorrow, all the zombies had been told, adjustments would be made, and then he and the others would get to rise from the grave.

*　*　*

In the morning, his fourth day on the set, Whisenant went directly to makeup. There had been rehearsals for the twelve of them who'd been hired to be zombies—how to stumble yet get somewhere, how to keep from blinking as much as possible, how to hold the body parts. "Chew the arms like turkey legs," the director said. "Hold the legs like ears of corn." But what Whisenant noticed, now that they were gathered in what looked to be an old grade school gym because the baskets were set at eight feet, there didn't seem to be enough zombies to overrun what was supposed to be an office building with as many as ten laboratories. "We'd need a shit load of zombies, that's for sure, if we were in the parking lot or in a field or a big room like this," the director admitted, "but the zombies won't come into any place wide open. Everything's inside this building once the zombies arrive, so a dozen of you coming down a narrow hall or barging into an office will look killer."

Whisenant asked one more question, this one about attrition. The zombies would be able to keep coming back for more, the director assured him, even after they were shot, because revival was cost efficient. Whisenant thought he remembered that a bullet to the brain always killed them for good. "That's been done," the director said. "These are new zombies. They're chemically enhanced. Nothing stops them unless they burn up."

Though it would make wonderful copy, Whisenant worried about being set on fire, especially on such a low budget, but the director explained that they'd burn in a group scene, out of sight except for establishing shots through windows and in rooms where the fire was just beginning. These zombies, the director went on, don't like bright light. They get confused and the fire engulfs them all. Because it would take place in a burning building, the flames consuming him and the others unseen by the audience, Whisenant would die safely for the final time because his destruction would be assumed rather than shown.

"We're doing the county a favor torching this place," the director explained. "This used to be where all the schools sent their retarded kids. Now they're all mainstreamed, and the place has gone to hell."

Whisenant noticed some of the other zombies glance at the basketball hoops as the makeup woman moved up beside the director. "We have, like, tons of different shirts and blouses for all of you," she began to explain. "Every time you're like, in a shot, you'll wear a different shirt. By the time we're done with you, there will be, like, twelve squared zombies in the building."

"We'll do some group shots first," the director said. "In the halls. In the lab. We'll use some of this, but let's get you all acting like zombies before we do the feeding scenes." For the rest of the day, Whisenant felt powerful in the makeup. Huge, in fact, but he didn't get into makeup again for the rest of the week. There was a hassle with lighting; there were complications obtaining the two police cars that had been promised for one of the few exterior scenes; the young woman who, it turned out, was scripted to survive had an asthma attack in the dust-filled janitor's closet where she hid during the first wave of zombie attacks.

Sitting in his car, Whisenant opened his laptop and worked the first of his articles into shape, finishing just as Amanda called his cell phone. "I want you to meet her," she said. "Lanie."

It was a sort of "yes" to answer "When?" but already Whisenant felt the way he had at meetings when he'd worked as a reporter, an hour dissolving into the liquid of the past because he didn't have the nerve to leave.

"Soon," she said. "Today, even."

"Where?"

"At the university," she said. "Lanie's in graduate school, too. Where did you think she was?"

Graduate school—it was something that struck Whisenant the way sleeping in did. "I needed that sleep." "It feels good to sleep in." He shuddered to hear those lines, like people were talking about stuffing their faces with cheap cookies, pleased to be giving in to useless feeding. All the graduate assistants he'd ever met thought they were going to work each day, but as far as Whisenant was concerned, they weren't.

His daughter was studying art. For a year and a half she had talked about painting rather than painted. "I will," she'd said four months ago, "when I'm ready." She laughed. "Eventually," she said, "in order to get my degree."

Just before she'd graduated from high school, Whisenant had told her how he'd gotten a newspaper job while he was still in college. It hadn't been hard to work full-time during his senior year. All he had to do was go to work at 4:00 p.m. instead of screwing around in a dorm or drinking or watching television. He hadn't taken a real test for two years, not one where you had to sit down and show you remembered something. Not one with a deadline of an hour and fifteen minutes after the problem was presented.

Finally, a month ago, Amanda had shown him her thesis project—nudes, female bodies, but in pieces. The paintings were close-ups of particular parts, so close up, in fact, that he had difficulty, for many of them, of telling which part of the flesh he was seeing. A portion of thigh, the back of an upper arm, the throat. Even one of a breast was so close that he'd mistaken the curve for the swelling of a stomach.

When he commented that the body parts looked like they came from different women, she said at once, "Because they did. I get a different model for each part."

He looked again, making distinctions about which of the women would be most attractive. The stomach excited him more than the breast, how it drew his eye down to the suggestion of pubic hair like an ad for jeans cut so low they said, "Want some?"

"I don't have feet or a vagina yet," she said. "No one's volunteered for those."

"Why are feet a problem?"

"They're not a problem. I just have to wait a bit more. I have a vagina model lined up. I just haven't had the time yet."

He thought of Georgia O'Keefe paintings and kept them to himself. Nothing about his daughter's work was going to couch itself in flowers. Of that he was sure.

"They're fascinating," he said, and she pressed her lips together.

"You can't say 'good,' can you?"

"They're better than good," he said at once, but she didn't smile.

"You're too late with that."

***

The zombies were excused early, nothing for them to do when they weren't in makeup, so Whisenant called Amanda. "OK," he said. "Let's do it," concentrating on maintaining the neutral tone of a lie detector cheat.

Half an hour later, his daughter led him through the fine arts building along a hallway lined with offices. He'd met three of the women his daughter had been intimate with. Each of them had been thin, but muscular in the way he'd always pictured ballerinas. Women who spent time each day in a fitness room. They made him think of child pornography, how their bodies, unclothed, would suggest thirteen-year-olds.

"She has an office upstairs," Amanda said. "We were in the same building for five months and never met."

Whisenant thought of how Lawrence might have looked in January. How long did you have to dress as a woman to pass the preoperative test?

They entered mixed-media, a small complex of offices among rooms full of electronic gizmos, the kinds of machinery Whisenant could never pay attention to except to notice light and sound. What they all had in common was an absence of realistic images or decipherable words. Everything was suggestion. He imagined conversations about theory, how gender and culture influenced the way a sequence of illuminated photographs of water indicated desire.

He noted, as he followed his daughter into an office, a temporary nameplate in one of the two slots. "Lanie Eyman," it read, just below a more permanent-looking one that said Sheila Jacobs.

"This is Lanie," his daughter said, beaming. Her stubbled hair made Whisenant think of a recruit at the end of boot camp. Lanie lifted one hand that hovered just above what Whisenant couldn't be sure were small, hormone-swollen breasts or subtle padding.

"Hi," he managed. Lanie looked like a beautiful boy in a skirt and blouse. When that thought occurred to him, it sounded inane, like a sort of sexist oxymoron. Relying on how at ease Lanie seemed to be, Whisenant estimated that the operation was going to be soon, and it occurred to him that if this scenario didn't include his daughter, he could write a week-long series about this man who was about to become a woman.

He could follow Lanie right down to the final days and then hours as if this was a variation of *Dead Man Walking*. How long did it take to recover from such an operation? When would the new body be ready to provide pleasure? Would there be remorse? Or terror?

"Amanda has told me you're a writer," Lanie said.

"Yes."

"The work you do sounds fascinating."

"Good." Whisenant heard himself turning monosyllabic the way he did in receiving lines. He searched the office for photographs, hoping to see a picture of Lawrence, but only Sheila Jacobs had photos on display, three pictures of a stocky young woman, posed in each with what looked to be a black Labrador retriever. Sheila looked sturdy enough to handle that dog.

"School bus driver was an upbeat one," he heard Amanda saying. "All those little kids from way out in the sticks turned out to be adorable." His daughter, Whisenant realized, was being generous, and he was grateful for the five minutes she kept things going until they left.

As they made their way back down the stairs, Amanda was animated. "See?" she said. "Isn't she something?"

"Have you known each other long?" Whisenant asked.

"More than a month," she said at once. "Thirty-nine days. Lanie says I'm keeping her focused."

"How's that?" Whisenant said, regretting the question at once.

"On her sex reassignment surgery. On the day when she becomes transsexual."

They were outside now, standing by his car. "I'm being a zombie," he said. "I'm in a horror movie for this article."

Amanda glanced back at the building as if she expected to see Lanie waving from a window. "Like *Night of the Living Dead* zombie?"

"Exactly. This one's called *Hazardous Waste*. A chemical company illegally dumps near a cemetery. You can guess the rest."

Amanda laughed. "That's wonderful," she said. "Is the makeup person good? Do you look dead?"

"I look awful," he said. "I look like I was smashed with the edge of a shovel."

"That's the way all those zombies look. Like they were murdered and buried by their killers."

"This is way low budget. I think most of their costs are in special effects. You'll get to read about it starting in a week or so. Almost all that's left are the zombie slaughter parts, and I've written the first two segments already. It's a six-part feature for the *Inquirer*. They want it to feel like I'm living it as I write it."

"It sounds cool."

"Bringiton.com won't steal this one," he said. "There's no cause to fight for."

"Yes, there is," Amanda said. "It has environmental issues."

***

As soon as he was alone again, Whisenant knew he wanted to save his daughter from what he believed was a terrible choice. To move in with a man who's about to forfeit his penis seemed like a black comedy skit on the homophobe channel. He was suddenly sure that Lawrence had already begun to grow breasts. He tried to imagine him in his house, sitting at the dinner table in a dress, but Whisenant couldn't see anything but how far the dress ran up Lawrence's thighs. When his cell phone rang, he saw it was Amanda, but he didn't answer. He placed it on the kitchen counter and walked through each room of his house as if he had been gone for weeks.

Upstairs, he opened a drawer in the dresser his wife had used and looked at the bras and panties and slips still neatly arranged there two years after her death. When he touched the silk and the lace, all of the lingerie that he had left there, just like the skirts and dresses in the closet, seemed like the whim of a stupid, sentimental fool.

Lawrence wasn't much different in height than Marie had been—five-seven, five-eight. Whisenant thought of him trying on his wife's clothes, and the image stuck in his throat like a piece of gristly, unchewed meat.

First, he pitched all of his wife's makeup into a waste can. He gathered the clothes together, filling garbage bags, beginning with his wife's underwear. It took him an hour to stuff everything into nineteen bags and load them into his van, and then he drove to the Goodwill site where there were dumpster-like bins and tossed everything away, two of the bags spilling open, scattering blouses and slips that he picked up from the pavement and flung on top of the jammed-in stack of bags. All that was left of his wife in their bedroom was her jewelry.

When he finished there were two messages on his cell phone. "Take tomorrow off," the first one said. "Nobody will be on the set at all. There were hassles at the bank." The other message was from Amanda, who invited him to dinner with

Lanie the following night. "Unless you're still a zombie, I'll pick you up around seven," she said.

***

He made himself a drink at 6:30, finished it, and had just made a second when Amanda arrived at quarter to seven. "It's OK, Dad," she said, glancing at the glass in his hand, "as long as we leave when it's gone."

Whisenant sipped the drink and waved the glass toward the stairs. "Tell you what," he said. "Since you're early, I want to show you something. It will only take a few minutes." He sipped again and carried the drink up the stairs, listening to hear if she was following.

He had arranged all of Marie's jewelry on the bed, dividing it into necklaces, bracelets, and earrings. He was surprised how much there was, like those times he put accumulated change into rolls before taking them to the bank. There was usually fifty dollars' worth, including several dollars' worth of pennies. Each time he wondered how he'd allowed so many coins to accumulate in the small pottery bowls Amanda had made in high school art.

"Do you want any of your mother's jewelry?" he asked her.

"I don't wear jewelry," she said. "You know that."

You did, he thought, when your mother was alive, but he kept himself on track. "Maybe someday you'll change your mind."

She jerked her head to the side as if he'd used a flash when he spoke. The necklaces and bracelets and earrings sparkled. Laid out on the bed, they looked stolen, like something to be divided among thieves.

"OK, Dad," she said. "I'll take them. They're like photographs, aren't they? It's like having pictures of Mom."

"Good," he said, but she'd given in so easily it seemed like a lie. He wanted to hold a necklace up to her, fasten it, and kiss her forehead. He could, if she were someone else, he thought, and he began to lay each piece into the jewelry box, knowing, unless his daughter died before he did, he was seeing them for the last time.

* * *

Lanie, it turned out, was already at the restaurant. Amanda sat beside him and dropped her coat on the chair across the table so that Whisenant had to sit facing Lanie, who, surprisingly, had a mug of beer in front of him. Immediately, Whisenant ordered a gin and tonic. "So," he said. "What's new?"

The phrase tumbled onto the table like a spilled drink.

Breasts, he thought, during the pause. Very soon, a cunt. He reached for his drink. Every sentence was dangerous.

"Like Amanda, I have a thesis to complete," Lanie finally said. "It's pressure time."

Whisenant had swallowed his drink like water. Holding the glass up as if the residue of ice might conceal worms, he looked for the waiter.

"Tell us about being a zombie, Dad. I told Lanie you get to eat people."

The waiter noticed and approached. "Gin and tonic?" he said, and Whisenant nodded. "Zombies are never satisfied," he said. "That's the first thing you learn. No matter how many arms and legs they chew on, they always want more."

"Some diet," Lanie said. "I guess there aren't any vegetarians." He kept his beer in his hand, drinking between sentences.

"That's right," Whisenant said. "Once you come back from the dead, you're a meat eater forever."

"But you never gain weight."

He saw the waiter coming with a fresh drink, but he already felt giddy. "Yes," he said. "It's wonderful. The women make pigs of themselves and keep their figures. No more exercise rooms."

Lanie laughed. "No more aerobics."

He was sure that Lanie had been drinking before they arrived. His daughter was silently picking at her salad. "Almost heaven," he said.

"West Virginia," Lanie sang at once, channeling John Denver, and they both laughed.

Before he could think, Whisenant said, "Amanda comes to my place for dinner every Thursday. You're welcome to accompany her."

***

Three more days went by with delays. He finished a third article and started the fourth, but numbers five and six were all about his action scenes, so he was relieved to get summoned back on Thursday.

"I've been seeing the feeding scenes," the director said. "You know—extended close-ups, special props." He held up what was unmistakably a heart, and Whisenant heard a few gasps, a smattering of laughs, and one muttered "Jesus Christ."

"Don't worry," the director said. "It's not from a morgue. It's a lamb's heart." He pointed with his heart-filled hand at a tall, middle-aged woman standing near Whisenant. "Sandy, I want you to be the zombie who slobbers all over this."

Sandy nodded, her eyes glued to the heart. "Rick," the director went on, nodding at Whisenant, "you're going to be our entrails-eating zombie."

Perfect, Whisenant thought, and he began to form sentences to take to the laptop as soon as he had a break. "We're only going to be showing four different zombies eating in close-up," the director said. "We think you'll be the ones who are really convincing with all the gore." Sandy raised one hand to her chest in a way that forced a laugh from the director. "Don't worry," he said. "The guts are on ice. We won't let them spoil."

Minutes later, Whisenant watched the actors who played Julie and George as they received instructions from the director. They were the last couple to die, the ones the audience was expected to feel most sorry for. George would be caught first, giving himself up so Julie and Greg and Samantha could escape, but unlike those other two, she'd stop and stare and scream while the zombies tore open his chest. So stupid, her behavior. George should have run for it while Julie was slaughtered. Now she tripped and fell. Now she hid herself in a room with no other exits but the one she'd entered through.

That would be it for Julie. Whisenant was the zombie who would step first through the broken door. All that was left for her was cowering in a corner. Tomorrow morning, the next minute in the script was to be his star moment.

* * *

Amanda was half an hour late. He'd cleaned up his papers and books from the dining room table and set three places, but when she opened the door, there was no one with her.

"It wasn't just the gin talking. Lanie is welcome for real," he said. "I should have sounded more sincere."

"We've had a falling out, Dad."

He felt such a surge of relief it was as if she'd called in the good news of surviving unscathed from an accident site.

"What's that mean?" he managed.

"She's been fucking around on me is what it means, Dad. She's been giving her ass to guys."

"I'm confused," he said.

"Aren't we all."

"I thought Lanie liked women."

"She says she's having second thoughts."

"I can understand that."

"That's such bullshit, Dad. She's not a transvestite."

He nodded, not ready to argue—because it was perfectly true. If there was something he didn't understand, it was the state of mind of a man who wanted his dick cut off. What he understood was that his daughter was devastated. "Lanie's a woman, Dad. She'll be unhappy the rest of her life if she doesn't go through with this. I told her I loved her."

For a moment the word emptied Whisenant of speech. He thought of the tongue he was going to tear from the mouth of a victim in the morning and pressed his own against the roof of his mouth until he felt the pressure run sideways through his jaw. "Have you ever thought of becoming a man?" he asked.

"No, Dad. Not at all."

"Really?"

He expected Amanda to slam the door and leave, but she didn't move or even raise her voice. "You don't get it, do you?" she said.

"It's a hard thing to get."

"It's just biology. It's like being left-handed. You just put the pencil in the hand that works and start writing." She was winding down, beginning to look at the place settings like someone who wished food on them to give her something to do with her hands and mouth. "It's such a guy thing," she said. "Lanie told me she couldn't help herself. What is she doing, Dad?"

What people have done since time began, he thought, the answer so obvious he couldn't bring himself to sadden her further by suggesting it. His daughter wanted case studies, not instinct, as evidence. "I was the one seeing her through all this," she said. "What could be more important?"

Pleasure, he thought, and he thought, too, of the guilt that wasn't regret that followed. "We're all selfish when it comes to our bodies," he said.

"The fuck we are," she said. When he didn't do anything but wait for her to go on, the rage went out of her. He watched her walk to the window and stare at the half acre of backyard that stretched to where it met the edge of the state game preserve.

She was breathing hard, nearly panting, and he let her concentrate on her heartbreak. Over her shoulders he could see the meadow his wife had talked him into, the high grasses, the tall, flowering plants he couldn't name, all of them reminding him of the weeds that flourished in abandoned lots.

What had become of that fad? He'd never seen another backyard given over to organized neglect, and without his wife to tend it, the yard seemed hopeless, something the township might send him a citation about, insisting he mow it or be fined.

He laid his hands on her shoulders and she flinched, startled, though she kept staring through the glass. He thought about wrapping his arms around her, but his hands, not moving, pushed slightly harder against her, a pressure he wanted her to notice. When she didn't turn or pull away, he felt such a longing he had to stare at the meadow to keep himself from crying.

All he could think of was how happy he would be now that his daughter would pair up with a natural woman. It seemed such an easy wish to make for her, but he knew she would be angry. If he hugged her, he was sure she would think it was out of a sense of duty.

* * *

The next morning, Whisenant hovered over Sandy as she raised the lamb's heart, showering the realistic-looking blood all over him before she tried to jam the heart into her mouth like a peach while Julie, still alive for now, screamed. After he changed his shirt, he waited until the director said, "This is your star turn. Rip her to shreds."

He lurched, remembering the hitch step he'd learned for his high school graduation. Step with the left, slide up the right. Step with the left, slide up the right. Except for chopping the length of his stride, it was the same way he'd marched to "Pomp and Circumstance."

Instead of getting to her feet and running again, Julie began to scream. Didn't she know her screaming was what attracted zombies? It was a sure sign you were alive. Zombies didn't eat each other. Zombies didn't speak.

Julie was on her feet now, but it was too late. His hands were on her shoulders. Her blouse had fallen open enough to show cleavage, but her breasts were to stay untouched. There were guts to be raised to his mouth after she kicked and struggled and fell to the floor.

As he clawed at her throat, he felt her body squirming under his for a moment. And then he knelt beside her, pawed at her stomach, and lifted intestines slick with blood, stuffing them into his mouth just as half of his fellow zombies arrived to join the feeding.

THE COMFORT OF TABOOS

"THE SECRET'S NOT TAKING THIS tournament too seriously," Brett Maslow advised when we were a mile outside of Corfu.

"I'm fine," I said. On the floor, between my feet, was a bowling ball I'd borrowed from the lanes where our faculty league threw three games every Friday after school. No matter what Maslow said, I intended to be serious. I wasn't going to show everybody what a novice I was by having to pick through a hundred house balls for one that was drilled with a hole large enough for my shovel-shaped thumb.

The scuffed ball was stuffed inside a small suitcase my wife Lorraine used to carry her "beauty stuff." I couldn't quite zip it shut, but at least I wouldn't have to carry the house ball in my hand when I walked into Corfu Lanes. Maslow's ball and his shoes were on the backseat, the ball inside a properly shaped Brunswick case with red and black stripes over a white background. It looked new, like maybe he'd bought it for this tournament, which was doubles, three games, total pins for the two of us. In January 1983, I was thirty-two years old, but I'd been bowling for only sixteen weeks, happy enough to have gotten my average up to 160 after starting out in the 140s. By now it didn't seem hard to bowl a 500 series, but everything above 550 had escaped me so far, and the word was that was the sort of score both Maslow and I would have to total if we expected to cash.

"Just picture yourself doing everything perfectly," Maslow said. "It helps more than you think." Outside, it had begun to snow, a promise of worse to come, but everybody in the faculty league except me was from upstate New York, and snow didn't slow them down unless the wind turned it sideways into a whiteout.

I taught juniors and seniors, but Maslow taught sixth grade, so I never saw him except during the two hours we spent bowling and drinking on Friday afternoons and when I sometimes drove his daughter Marlene home after she babysat for Lorraine and me, watching over Beth and Brady, our seven- and nine-year-old girls. Marlene was seventeen, and since September she'd sat so quietly in my British Literature class that her voice still sounded odd when she spoke. "Reliability isn't a function of personality," Lorraine said every time she was pleased to come home and find our children safe and happy. Marlene had never opened a can of the soda we left for her in the refrigerator. She had never touched the potato chips or cookies. If she had tended the girls full-time, they might never have eaten anything but fruits and vegetables. Even better, the girl had a younger sister, fourteen, who we expected would become a replacement sitter by the next fall when Marlene went off to college.

Scattered among the thirty-six teams starting at seven o'clock were eight other guys from our league bowling in pairs. A handicap tournament, seventy percent of the difference between your average and 200, so it didn't seem to matter I'd been paired with Maslow, who had an average nearly identical to mine. Only Roy Lentz and Ted Leckey had averages over 170 in our league, less than ten pins difference in our handicap scores. "Stay calm," Maslow said as I readied myself for my first shot, one that came up thin on the head pin and left the 2-4-7 for me to convert. "Relax," Maslow said, beginning to make me understand why I'd been stuck with him, but I picked up the spare and sat down without a word.

Maslow hooked his first ball left of the head pin, leaving the 1-3-6-10. "A lot of oil on these lanes," he said while he waited for his ball to return, and I nodded as if I had any idea what that meant.

He missed the spare and then another in the second and the third. It looked to me like he was holding onto the ball too long before he released it. "Maslow giving you his best?" Roy Lentz said, leaning over my shoulder to whisper while Maslow hooked another ball to the left of the head pin.

"So far, so bad," I said.

Lentz seemed to study Maslow as he readied himself for his fourth frame. "He's a piece of work. It's no wonder he's down there in the grade school with the babies."

"I guess I'm fucked," I said, and Lentz grinned, carrying that assessment back to where he and Ted Leckey were already sixty pins ahead of us after three frames. By the time Maslow filled a frame in the fifth, our team was as good as eliminated from having a chance to cash. I bowled a 522, a little over my average, but Maslow, after his opening 116, barely broke 400, a miserable performance, one that kept him quiet in the car. That and the heavy snow, the twenty mile drive taking nearly an hour with Lorraine's travel bag between my feet on the soggy floor.

Because Lorraine substituted in the grade school, the news about Maslow came home with her the following Thursday. "I'm in MaryJo Bryce's room, fourth grade, right across the hall from Jolene Fawcett, and she's in and out of her room three times in an hour, so I had to ask, and she gives me a look, you know, like it's not the flu that has Danny Rohr, the principal, in Brett Maslow's room all afternoon."

Lorraine glanced past me down the hall. "Where are the girls?" she said. "In their rooms?"

"Yes," I said, and I knew by her asking that Maslow's career was over.

"They're trying to keep it quiet," she said, "but there's no sitting on something like this." She looked down the hall again before she went on. "There's been accusations. From three girls."

"Accusations?"

"Inappropriate touching."

"In his room?"

"Yes. Three girls, so there's corroboration already, and this is just getting started, you can bet on that."

***

By the weekend the story was in the local newspaper. Maslow had been put on paid leave "until this is resolved," the superintendent was quoted, as if there was the slightest chance Maslow would be allowed back in the classroom. Near the end of the article the reporter acknowledged that Maslow had denied the accusations, all of his comments in summary rather than directly quoted. The last paragraph declared that no one else but the original three girls had come forward.

"Maybe those girls don't like Maslow," I said. "Maybe they're making it up to ruin him."

Lorraine looked at me. "Maybe he's been doing this for a good long while is more like it. He's been teaching for what, twenty years?"

"Something like that."

"He didn't just start this year, you can count on that."

"So when?"

"When his daughters got too old."

I wondered at Lorraine's anger, how she was leaping from what might have been an overzealous teaching technique on Maslow's part to believing him capable of incest. "How could he?" I said.

"Because he could. Because they were there." She said it as if she knew Marlene and her sister had testified under oath.

"There's something built into us to keep that from happening," I said.

"Really? Then Brett Maslow is missing the gene that keeps us from evil."

***

There was no point in arguing, but I didn't give up hoping Maslow wasn't the guy he sounded like, that those girls really did just have it in for him or that they were doing it on a dare, something you think up at a sleepover. I didn't say that out loud to anybody, but I remembered how once, in the school where I'd taught before, a girl, angry about her grade, had said,

"I should tell somebody you touched me. That would serve you right."

The snotty bitch, I'd thought after she'd left my room. That's what I remembered now, how that phrase came to me and stayed for the rest of the school year every time I saw her. The girl was fifteen, and I was sure she'd told her friends about her threat to let them know how she'd put me in my place.

"A piece of work"—I remembered Lentz's observation from the Corfu Lanes. Maslow was one of those teachers that students sensed was weak. "Effeminate," they might have said, had they been older. A "wuss" is what they likely said. Or worse. He was so slight and small and meek-voiced I imagined those students, young as they were, testing him since September, and by now, late January, he'd be teetering into the second semester just barely in charge.

The eleven-year-old boys wouldn't challenge him outright, but they would talk back. Lorraine had remarked a few times before Christmas that there was constant chatter coming from Maslow's room. Walking past the closed door, she said, you might hesitate, thinking the teacher had left the room and those sixth-graders were unattended.

Maslow didn't have size. He didn't have a voice. I imagined Maslow being nervous all day, never quite in control. I imagined him telling himself each year that this time it would be different, that he'd stop being so passive.

Presence. It's what you needed, even if it was as contrived as meting out punishment exactly as you promised, never varying until even the louts saw the futility of not complying. Because laying a hand on them was taboo.

The next weekend, when Lorraine told Maslow's daughter we didn't need her to babysit like she did every other Saturday, I could tell from how quickly Lorraine hung up the phone that Marlene hadn't even asked why we'd changed our minds, but I murmured, "For God's sake," when Lorraine came back into the living room.

"For our sake is more like it," she said. "For Beth and Brady's sake. Don't you know molested children are more likely to molest?"

"What's next?" I said, "Burn down his house?" but I gave her the names of two girls in my classes who I thought would be good.

"We're all set," Lorraine said five minutes later. She stood over me as I slouched on the couch. "Did you know there was another teacher here five years ago who took pictures of his students? Fourth grade. Beth's age. This isn't new here."

"Teachers take pictures of their students all the time."

"Not one by one. Not lying down. Jeff Orton. You ask around. And then you tell me why he's still teaching somewhere just because this school was so happy to see him go that they didn't put anything about it in his file." She looked triumphant. "So they can't sit on this one. Not a bit. It's all in the paper if you ever get around to reading it."

"What's new?"

"They found pictures at Maslow's house."

"Pictures?"

"Don't play dumb. You know what I'm talking about. Those kinds of pictures."

I thought of Jeff Orton's fourth graders lying on the carpet in his room, what angles he would shoot from.

"What a creep," Lorraine said.

"Where were the pictures?"

"In his house. What do you mean 'where?'"

"Where do you hide something like that? You'd have to believe they'd never be found, not ever."

"They didn't say."

The garage, I thought, some place where only a man goes, on the back of a shelf full of power tools or fertilizer bags or weed killer. Where did Maslow get the pictures? When did he look? Late at night? It was winter half the year in upstate New York, so it seemed as if he wouldn't go to the garage. It would be when the house was empty. When he knew for certain he wouldn't be surprised. He'd bring those pictures inside and spread them around him on his bed.

* * *

Maslow's daughter, for the next three days, sat sideways in her desk, as if she needed space to stretch her legs. She faced the windows, reminding me of my wife when she watched television on mute while she talked on the phone.

The third day she sat like that I thought it was because she was poised to bolt. The previous two days I'd passed over her for answers, calling on everybody at least once like I always did, but now I said "Marlene?" in what I hoped was a comforting tone.

"I don't know," she said, though the question was a simple one, the sort I offered to my weakest students.

"George?" I said at once to the boy across from her, relieved that she hadn't stood up or screamed. I noticed two boys near the front turn sideways in their seats. When a third boy, sitting just in front of Marlene, turned as well, I wrote a sentence on the board. "Ray," I said to the boy who'd just turned, "take a close look at this," but Marlene had already put her head down on her desk, contorted from the side, her shoulders quivering to the rhythm of what I was certain were muffled sobs.

It would be better to have your father accused of murder, I thought. Much better. Those boys would be entranced, but none of them would imagine Maslow killing Marlene the way they were seeing her body being used when they were in the elementary school.

* * *

Maslow had trouble converting spares. That's what I remembered now when I thought about the sixteen Fridays of bowling. He threw a slow hook, a ball that curved more than anyone's in the league, but he threw his spare ball the same way, something Lentz had told me was a bad idea. "Straight on," he'd suggested the first week I bowled, and since I knew he'd carried the highest average the previous year, I gave it a try, even when Maslow, later that afternoon, said it was best to throw every ball exactly the same. "That way you don't have to think," he said. He'd been bowling for twenty years and was no better than I was after four weeks. By then I listened to Lentz until I learned he always had wisdom to offer with such inflexible certainty nobody ever challenged him.

This time it was "Where there's smoke, there's fire" that Lentz declared in the faculty lounge. A ripple of silence spread out from where he was standing. None of us wanted to be the first person to weigh in on degrees of guilt, but I'd just watched Marlene cry for the last ten minutes of class, so I hazarded a response.

"Maybe not," I said, figuring that observation for nearly harmless. I hadn't known Jeff Orton, the teacher who'd taken suggestive pictures, and maybe that made it easier for me to decide he was worse, that a man who took pictures was more guilty than a man who just looked at them and hadn't yet been convicted of putting his hands on a girl.

I kept that to myself, sticking exclusively to Maslow's case, but Lentz looked at me, and I understood he wanted to tell me more than I was wrong, that he thought maybe I was a man capable of rationalizing some perversion of his own. He went stiff, like he was being introduced to a family at a funeral. "You have the inside dope on this?" he said. "You the school expert on short eyes?"

"Pictures might be proof," I said, "but an accusation is just that—an accusation."

"A thief's a thief; a perv's a perv."

"You sound like Confucius," I said. "Like somebody who should be wearing a sheet."

I meant it to sound brittle, or even better, steely, but Lentz smiled and said, "So, fuck you, I do," and nobody chimed in.

I didn't press on. The odds were against me, and I'd always been someone who acted as if he was willing to buck them until it could cost me more than I was willing to risk. Saying anything more might make my life more difficult than the one I'd already formed. I didn't need Roy Lentz to make that clear, but right then I was ready to go back to another section of my British Literature seniors and talk about Keats and Shelly and all the rest of the Romantics that the girls, at least, adored. "Maslow's fucked one way or the other," I said, "that's for sure," and no-body disagreed because there was nothing that could change the minds of the men I worked with.

Lentz grinned then, dropping into a chair. "One thing's for sure," he said, "Maslow will be better for your team by not showing up. He'll get fifteen pins below his average per game for the rest of the year, more than he'd bowl if he was actually there."

"He knows his shit stinks now," Ted Leckey said. "He can smell it, the little prick."

These men had known Maslow for years. I tried to dismiss their contempt as rage at being deceived, but I thought, sud-denly, their anger was because they weren't surprised, that they recognized weakness in themselves at allowing Maslow the benefit of the doubt until three eleven-year-old girls gave them the muscle to heave him overboard.

I'd heard Leckey and Lentz describe their students' bodies explicitly. It was as if a line was drawn at the beginning of the junior year, that after that it was natural to fantasize. Somebody had worked that border into place over time, and I thought that ten years ago, when I'd started teaching, the line was when the girls became seniors. If Maslow had been close to either line, sophomores, say, opinions might have been different.

***

What do we expect from ourselves? That there are things we're convinced we'd never do? That's what Roy Lentz wanted to make clear. I knew that. But what I couldn't say was we needed the comfort of taboos. If Roy and my wife saw the sense of that, they wouldn't admit it, and neither should I. It was enough to manage another day without surprising myself with flaws in character.

The school library had two shelves full of old yearbooks. I'd looked through a few from ten or twelve years before, checking out pictures of men like Leckey and Lentz when they were just out of college in the early seventies with sideburns and long hair. I was glad nobody had access to the yearbooks from my first job—a turtleneck, mutton chops—the pictures made me ask why I had been hired.

Now I chose a yearbook from six years ago and turned to sixth grade. There stood Maslow with his class. He looked the same, one of those guys who seems forty-five when he's thirty. I didn't recognize Marlene in any of the five sixth-grade rooms, so I had to check the names that ran underneath each photo until I found her, counting four in from the left, third row, and seeing her tall and thin, her hair cut short so I could have taken her for a boy in her striped, flared pants and wide-collared blouse.

I tried to imagine her wearing that outfit and walking past Maslow in his house, what he thought as he looked at her, but nothing came to me. It seemed impossible for a father to be aroused by his eleven-year-old daughter.

I knew what I was doing, trying to understand the urgency in my wife's voice, how there was an impatience in it beyond my own recognition that Maslow was wrong. For her, that wasn't enough. I was supposed to want to beat Maslow with my fists; short of that was acceptance.

* * *

On Sunday, Beth and Brady wore the identical dresses Lorraine had sewn for them for Christmas. It was February now, and the dresses seemed new again, deep green and trimmed in silver along the sleeves. Though it wasn't a special Sunday, the church looked packed, dozens of families sitting together, half of them, it seemed, with eleven-year-old daughters who wore dresses that ended above their knees.

I noticed Lorraine looking at me. "What?" I said the second time.

"You're my husband," she said. "Wives look at their husbands when they're together."

It sounded wrong. When we'd dated I'd never stopped looking at her. It started with children, I thought. They were what you looked at. They ran ahead each time you slowed. They babbled anything at all, and you turned your head to listen.

I tried to busy myself with the church bulletin, which had a picture of Jesus surrounded by children on its cover. I folded it so the picture was inside and jammed it between the hymns on pages 386 and 387. An hour later I left it stuck in the hymnal when I placed it back in the wooden rack as the recessional hymn ended.

When Beth saw that the two-day-old snow pack on the sidewalk had turned to slush during the service, she asked me to carry her. "Sure," I said, swinging her up over my head to hear her squeal before I settled her in the crook of my arm.

"Me too?" Brady said at once. "Me too?" I shifted Beth into my left arm and lifted Brady, balancing the two as we started the five block walk to our house.

"Pretty soon we'll be so big you can't hold both of us at the same time," Beth said.

"Pretty soon, but not yet."

Even with their winter coats on, they felt light enough to carry the whole way, but the last two blocks were uphill, and the sidewalks, in the shadows of houses, were slick with packed snow in spots. "Down you go," I said.

They scampered ahead, but Lorraine didn't close up beside me. OK, I told myself. OK. And then I cursed Maslow and his pictures and his inappropriate touching, wishing he'd gone out and raped a girl so nothing in my behavior would have anything to do with him.

* * *

Lorraine waited until 9:30, when both girls were asleep, before she brought up Maslow again. "Don't you think it's helplessness that excites a man like that?" Lorraine said.

"I don't know," I said, which was the truth, but her lips flattened out toward the start of a snarl.

"Yes, you do," she said. "You know what he's thinking. It's because they're so young and so small."

I thought I knew what my wife was afraid of. Not that I was capable of doing the things Maslow had done, but that I was someone who could let the world return to normal like a man turning off a television show.

"Have you ever thought about it?" Lorraine said.

"What?"

"You know."

"Touching them?"

"Or more." She looked anxious, like she was worried that it was possible.

"No," I said, and she smiled. I'd told the truth because she'd only asked about the young girls Maslow taught. And maybe that was enough for her, not wanting to ask about the sixteen- and seventeen-year-olds I saw each day, an impossible thing not to think about.

"Men like that," she said, "they kill the children they rape to keep them from telling."

"Touching isn't rape," I said.

"What makes you think so?"

"Because it isn't."

Lorraine backed away from me as if she needed distance from my words. "If I even suspected you had those thoughts, I couldn't live with you."

"It's one weakness I don't have."

"I wouldn't be able to look at you." Her face had turned tight, but there was nothing I could do to soften her but let her anger exhaust itself. All I had were denials, not nearly enough.

"I'd want to kill you," she said at last. "I'm sure of that. Rid the world of you."

She puffed her cheeks and blew out a breath, something I took for a signal, and then she wrapped her arms around me and whispered, "You know I'm right," directly into my ear, delivering that sentence like a lover.

So I felt smaller, like that moment when you begin to realize you're shrinking into the shape old age will give you, and when I didn't immediately say, "Yes," Lorraine's expression made me feel as if she'd learned something terrible about me. She looked revolted.

I understood that she had never expected anything from me but agreement that Maslow deserved to be loathed—"discussion ended," as she put it to our daughters when her patience wore out for their whining about schoolwork or dinner or the length of a car trip. I was a person who didn't think Maslow was evil, no questions asked. And then I recognized that it wasn't revulsion she felt. She was terrified.

***

Maslow must have woken up every day telling himself to stop. If he didn't believe that, he wouldn't be able to get through the day. Nobody wants to be a pedophile. There's not much worse than that. The guilt would be like a hangover, even for just looking at pictures. You'd make vows and pledges and maybe even throw all the pictures away, the house feeling clean and your life taking a turn for the better. But every day you'd look at the girls in your class and remember what you'd imagined yourself doing when those pictures were spread out around you.

You'd have to burn the pictures. You couldn't throw something like that in the garbage. Once, when I was thirteen, I'd found a magazine in the woods near my house. It was full of pictures of naked women. I'd never seen anything like it, and I'd stood behind a tree the way I'd done a hundred times to piss and jerked myself off onto the ground. I'd stuffed that magazine under a nearby log.

I'd come back the next day, but the magazine was gone. The memory of it had made me hard again. I'd looked on the ground for my semen, but it was gone, too. Suddenly, I thought somebody could be watching me, and yet I jerked off again.

***

After Lorraine went to bed, I stayed up, not doing anything but sitting on the couch waiting for her to fall asleep. After fifteen minutes of this I opened a cabinet in the dining room where we kept old photo albums, including one of each of us from before we knew each other. I looked at Lorraine as a baby. Lorraine as a toddler. Lorraine as an elementary school student. Lorraine, finally, as a sixth grader. My eyes went to her flat chest and small hips. I felt like a predator. I thought about summer when I'd see girls like her in bathing suits, their bodies practically naked, and I stuffed that album back into the cabinet and went to the window to look out at the bare branches of trees, the spongy earth, a few small patches of gray snow that would be gone when I walked home tomorrow.

I told myself that seeing those girls differently was like learning I was sure to die. Or like discovering God wasn't a certainty. I'd adjusted to those. This was one more thing to get used to. It might take a while, but I had to believe it would happen.

***

It turned out Maslow didn't have pictures that were outright pornographic, not naked ones, or even half-naked, just a few hundred pictures of preteen girls in clothes, something you'd have to supplement with fantasies to make them sick. Jeff Orton, the teacher who'd taken pictures, was married just like Maslow, and the girls in his photos were nine or ten years old. None of them were naked or even half-naked either. But he had hundreds of photos, and those numbers and the poses of those girls seemed to undress them.

What did Maslow do? Make up stories about the girls he looked at until he was so aroused he couldn't finish another thought without touching himself? Did he need to make up new fantasies each time or could he just rely on the old stories? It might not even have been technically illegal, though it was plenty enough to get him fired because the clothes didn't lessen disgust, but when the description of the photos appeared in the newspaper, I heard myself say, "He had restraint at least." It was the best I could do for Maslow, one audible rationalization for not wanting to beat him into a hospital stay.

Immediately, Lorraine said, "I hope you don't mean that."

"You're right," I said. Indefensible. There was a time for that word, and it had arrived.

"Thank you." Her tone was so withering and dismissive I had to leave the room without saying another word. My wife, under the same circumstances, had already convinced me she would want to kill me. Thank you, I said to myself, the tone I imagined so soft and grateful that it came to me like a reiteration of love, a gratitude for her absolute disgust and rage.

* * *

The only time I saw Maslow again he was shoveling snow. Something small and ordinary, and yet I paused half a block away and watched him shoveling his driveway. In upstate New York, where winters were deep with snow, almost everybody owned a snow blower or small plows, but Maslow was lifting and throwing in the sort of rhythm that called up the possibility of heart attack.

To work off his energy—I heard my mother's phrase come back to me from when I was in junior high school. She'd meant me to keep busy so I wouldn't be playing with myself. She thought a twelve-year-old could be so exhausted he wouldn't masturbate as soon as he was alone.

Now the phrase seemed as appropriate and futile as it had been twenty years ago. Back then I'd thought about girls the whole time I was cutting the grass or weeding the garden. There were times I opened my pants in the garage when I was putting the lawnmower away, finishing in a few seconds, smearing the goop with my shoe until the stain looked like it might have come from oil.

Maslow noticed me and paused. It was up to me to call out a greeting, but all I managed was a brief wave, ending it by tugging at my hat as if the cold had just then begun to bother me.

Maslow didn't wave. He held the shovel across his body like a rifle, and as I passed, half a driveway's length away, I thought his face seemed different, that now he didn't have to be Brett Maslow, the teacher. I thought it was a kind of rehearsed hardness, something practiced and cynical. But once I'd passed I thought it was the ugliness of rage, what a man might show before he swung that shovel at the head of another man.

It was all I could do to keep from turning my head. No, it was all I could do to keep from running.

THE VISUAL EQUIVALENT OF PAIN

How many times have I heard some guy say, "I want to kill the bitch?"

For sure, more than I can count on my fingers. But not lately, not since I turned forty and had fewer friends who got drunk and ranted. So it sounded ominous when Frank Wertz, fifty-one years old, made that declaration less than two hours into drinking nothing but beer, long before he had the excuse of his brain turning to mush.

Frank Wertz was hating his ex-wife so much in words he looked up at the sky as if he wanted God to hear better. Sam Pagala and I looked up too, taking in all those ancient patterns, suggestions from the imaginations of people so long dead it felt like we were sharing something important for a minute the way a six pack works on the ordinary.

We were standing in Frank's backyard a year after Sharlene had left him for a man she'd been sleeping with for months. A year. It had been so long he caught us by surprise with his threat. He had the windows open and the speakers near them so the "misery mix," tunes he'd burned onto a CD especially for tonight, pumped into the yard. It had started with a song Sam and I didn't know called "I Hate Everything about You," but once that was over the rest of the tunes sounded familiar: "The World is a Ghetto," "Backstabbers," "You're So Vain," all the angry songs from 1972 when Frank would have been sixteen or seventeen like us and maybe muttering aloud to his high school friends about what he wanted to do to some girl who'd turned down his invitation to the prom. On either side of us the neighbors' houses were dark, but we'd started so late it was nearly time for someone to call the police, something that Sam, with twenty-eight years on the force, had pointed out half an hour earlier when Frank had taken the cooler of beer into his backyard.

There had been six of us before we'd followed Frank outside, but three had considered their drives home, what it took to manage without incident, and opted for leaving. Sam and I lived in town, a mile or so, a few stop signs and streets narrowed by parked cars, routes we'd managed through years of drinking with Frank, who loved to host in the summer because it meant he could choose the music that worked as a soundtrack for his stories about camping and canoeing and hiking trails where the state park explorers never ventured.

Those stories always came last, a signal that the night was slowing down, all of us holding our last beer, because only Sam was an outdoorsman among us. So we could leave, the rest of us, mid-excursion, without insulting Frank, those of us who took our hikes on treadmills in local fitness centers and used rowing machines if we wanted to paddle without worrying about how deeply or swiftly the water ran underneath us.

Frank kept a set of free weights in his basement, a weightlifting bench set up so the stereo washed directly over him as he worked out without a spotter. He didn't tell stories about what he could bench press or dead lift, and that made his stories about isolation and danger easier to take, something like Sam restraining himself when the world's weaknesses were the subject, talking more about places and people than he did about the crimes. We all knew Frank could double our bench press limit; we all knew Sam had seen the results of gunshots and knives and knotted stockings.

What else we had in common was we were the three men among us whose marriages had failed. It seemed natural for the others to break off and go home, like those huge chunks of ice that tumble off the edges of glaciers and drop into the ocean.

Sam had been divorced twice, which seemed to show he'd made his peace with failure. Once, shortly after Sharlene had left, Frank had asked Sam and me what had ruined our marriages. "Fucking other women," Sam had said at once, smiling.

We'd been in Frank's living room with the television tuned to a basketball game on mute. The image flickered in my peripheral vision because I'd moved to a chair that faced away from the screen. Frank and Sam looked past me half the time, keeping track of the game, but now Frank stared at me, waiting.

I glanced back at the television. A commercial for a telephone company was on, the one with the nerdy guy repeating, "Can you hear me now?" a slogan I'd heard customers repeat inside the library every day for nearly a year, making me hate them. Frank held his stare.

"Boredom," I'd finally said.

Frank nodded and drank from his beer. "Sure," he'd said. "Sure fucking thing."

Now Frank looked at both of us. "I'm in a terrible fix here," he said.

I hoped Sam would offer advice, even something useless like, "Give it time," but all he did was bring his bottle to his mouth like there was something left in it besides an excuse for silence.

"I feel like I've shrunk. You know, like people can tell I'm smaller the way anybody over thirty looks when they're doing one of those shit jobs like stocking shelves or delivering pizzas. You know, you see them in the fucking grocery store all hunched over beside a cart full of cereal boxes or canned soup; they're fucking disappearing right there as you pass by them."

"The sky does that to you," I said, and right away I wished I hadn't because Frank looked at me in a way that made me turn my head.

We all stood there then. Sam's car was behind mine in the driveway, so he needed to leave first. There was no way I could be the next to speak, but I felt lucky not to be Frank.

"So many stars," Frank said, finally shutting up about Sharlene. He kept looking skyward, but after being his friend for ten years, I knew he didn't think anything was there but animals like or unlike us. "Some of them are looking our way," he said, "but they sure as hell aren't raising the dead and tending them like sheep."

His voice went hoarse, the way talking takes your words after a while on the late night road to silence. "You ever smack your head hard enough on something to see stars?" he said.

"Yeah," Sam said while I was trying to remember if I'd ever actually done that or just seen the stars hovering around the heads of a hundred comic book characters who'd banged their head on something.

"You know what those are? They're the visual equivalent of pain."

Sam didn't say anything and neither did I. The misery mix ended, and suddenly the backyard was so quiet I remembered watching the stars at the Buhl Planetarium in Pittsburgh when I was a boy, how the chairs tilted back like I was at the dentist and this voice spoke as if it were talking from the sky, giving instructions about distance and time while I gave in to wonder.

* * *

The next day I was at the hospital, regretting the night before and feeling sorrowful about my prospects. The barium shake I was forcing down tasted like the terrible strawberry of the bubble gum that drops out of the machines in convenience stores; I had half a cup to go when I saw Sharlene standing in the doorway.

She looked at the cup in my hand. "You having an upper GI?" she said.

"Yes."

"You have a problem?"

"Let's hope not." I'd complained about heartburn to my doctor. Every day, I'd said, not saying anything about how I'd kept thinking I had a heart problem until I got so used to it I knew it was something else.

"Women in uniforms"—the fetish-site phrase came to me as she took a step into the room. For a moment my apprehension was muted by the distraction of her body. She wasn't a beautiful woman, but she was a woman a lot of men would think about wanting to get into bed with if they saw her. A young-looking forty. I thought it was because she'd never had babies, but she looked fit, like if you unbuttoned her nurse's outfit and saw her stomach, that it would look like a girl's, smooth and flat and slightly rounded as it takes the start of that breathtaking curve under the waist band.

Maybe it was because Frank was past fifty like I was and Sam was, so she had the advantage on us. "All these machines we have," she said. "They can see every last inch of us."

"I bet."

"Sometimes I think I'll see somebody's soul. You know. It has to be someplace inside you; it's just a matter of time before we'll be able to see its condition like any organ's." I didn't put much faith in that possibility, the best reason I had for going through this exam. "You'll do good on your test. You'll see."

"I hope you're right about that."

"Your color's good. You'd be surprised how much you can learn from just that one thing."

"I would be," I said. "There's no doubt about that."

She looked behind her into the hall where I couldn't see and then back again. "I have to go," she said, though I could tell she hadn't seen anyone, that she'd just run up against the end of things to say about my health.

"Of course," I said. "You're working, and I'm just visiting."

She smiled, but she'd already taken two steps back, her body outside the door. "Well then." I could hear something on wheels coming down the hall, but the sound stopped before anything passed by the space I could see.

She paused for a few seconds, resting a hand on the door frame before she spoke again. "What's' the weather like on Hudson Street?" she said. "You know?"

"Cloudy."

"I'll bet."

"Then you know already."

"I guess that's true."

After Sharlene disappeared, I had nothing to do but listen closely to the burning in my chest, what had brought me to the hospital after it had reappeared every day for three months. I'd looked up the choices for what I felt and where that discomfort was located. Acid reflux was the good one, the kind of problem that's just an embarrassment. The other choices were ones that would change me forever—ulcers, or worse, cancer. They called up every eating and drinking vice I had, from greasy food to all-day beer. And it didn't miss my notice that cancer of the esophagus had a miserably high percentage of killing you within five years.

* * *

Two days later I had good news. All I had to do was be sensible when I ate, buy a giant-sized bottle of Tums, and prop myself up in bed. I thought of celebrating with a cheeseburger and fries, but I roamed the aisles of the grocery store looking for items that said fat-free. I can do this, I said to myself, though the choices were bleak, the packages covered with the words *baked* and *lean* and *soy*.

I microwaved the best of the lot—low-fat chicken with Chinese vegetables and rice—and settled down in front of the noon news. "Breaking News" was flashing on the bottom of the screen, the announcer describing the kidnapping of a woman from the hospital where she worked as a nurse. "Believed to be her estranged husband," the announcer said. "At gunpoint."

There was a standoff in progress as I began to watch, and when the overhead shot zoomed in, I knew enough about the make and model of the car to eliminate all of the other nurses and put Sharlene inside that green Plymouth with Frank.

There was concern about the woman's condition. The police were there in force, still talking with "the suspect" when the on-site reporter declared a shot had been heard. The announcer described the police movement as "cautious advancement." I poked at the broccoli and carrots and tiny, brittle pieces of chicken with my fork until an ambulance pulled up, and I could see Frank and who I figured for Sharlene being taken away.

I sat in front of the television for another hour, but there weren't any more updates. I kept wanting to open a beer, but I stayed downstairs with my cold, ready-made healthy dinner, and stared at the soap opera that ended and was replaced by another. I looked away then, focusing on the hundreds of CDs I had arranged on two shelves that were built into one wall of my basement above the television. Frank loved the way they were ordered from soft and slow to loud and aggressive. "By fucking mood," he'd said once. "What a great fucking library for sound. You ought to do this where you work and let people know where the books are for when they're sad or happy or pissed."

"The best books cover everything," I'd said.

"That's a short shelf then," Frank had said. "That's one you could empty with one hand."

For a few minutes, I thought I wanted to play something aggressive but sad, but all of the titles made me think of those times in a music store when I'd gotten depressed and decided there was no point in ever buying even one more CD.

I didn't want to slip into wanting to throw them through the window into the yard, something I'd done once with half of my collection of vinyl, relieved, the following morning, to find only a handful of the records had skidded out of their sleeves. So I walked out the back door and away from anything of my own I might harm.

For a while I just hiked fast, surprised how long it took to get away from houses. As I walked, I imagined my wife unfaithful, her making a choice for the other man. The humiliation. My anger.

I've kept a gun in my house since the day I moved in with my wife and two sons. The gun, I told Helen, came with owning something so large, the need to protect it. When she threatened to throw it into the river, I explained to Helen that it was taped to the underside of the bed where the boys wouldn't see it, but my hand could find it coming out of sleep to an awareness of an intruder.

Once the boys were grown and gone, Helen hadn't complained about the gun being there. She never mentioned it or anything else she disapproved of until she'd filled her van with boxes and suitcases and stood in the driveway with the van idling to say, "It's all yours, Harry. Now you can put your pistol under your pillow like James Bond."

Facing traffic, I thought I was going to imagine shooting her, but nothing showed up in my head. Nothing whatsoever except the darkness of anticipation, what it might be like before being born.

Big thoughts. That's what my father would have called my ideas—getting into territory for which you're not equipped. "You're getting things inside that head of yours that it's not large enough to hold," he'd say. "All this mooning around won't get you anywhere."

My father had done the same thing as I did when I was thirty years old—built a house in the country and seen it surrounded in five years when three farmers sold their land to developers. The year I was nine, that second summer, just before building began, he'd taken me through what he knew would be the last crop of corn. It was August, the corn as high as it would get. He must have known I'd be frightened walking among the stalks in the dark.

The field was full of rustling and scurrying noises that made me stop to look down so often he said, "The things that live here aren't interested in you, Harry."

After a while we came out of the corn into a bare space where rocks were scattered. Some of them were enormous, ten feet long, six feet thick. "How many tons do you think they weigh?" he asked.

"Ten," I answered at once, and when he said, "Guess again," I knew my answer was foolish.

"A hundred."

"Maybe."

"A thousand."

My father climbed onto the largest stone and lifted me up so we could see over the top of the corn in every direction. "Look at this," he said, but all I saw was corn all the way to faint lights where I thought the houses on our street had to be.

He kept standing there, not speaking, and I slid down to scramble over the rocks as if I was exploring on another planet. A minute later, I stepped on a stone that shifted under my weight and turned my ankle. I sat on a boulder and held it. "Oh

Christ," my father said, climbing down. "Put your weight on it. Walk it off."

I worked to keep from crying and limped into the corn, following him. I kept falling behind, and he would slow for a few seconds, but never stop. I was panicked. If I lost sight of him I thought I would be lost forever.

It took a long time to get through the corn. Maybe half an hour with me hobbling like I did. When we emerged and saw the six houses on our street, I sat down where our lawn began and listened to the pain flooding up my leg. Now that I didn't have to keep up, I wanted to crawl to our back door. "See?" my father said. "See what you can do when you have to?"

A rustle in the field I was passing snapped me out of remembering so fast I nearly lurched sideways onto the highway. Just some animal, I said to myself, but I kept an eye on the swaying weeds until the traffic thinned enough for me to cross the road. When the news report came on at five o'clock, it said that Sharlene was dead.

***

He had sex with her before he shot her, the newspaper said the following morning, and Sam confirmed it. "In the fucking backseat," he said. "Like they were at the drive-in or something." I stood in the doorway to the kitchen. Behind me, on the counter, a package of skinless turkey cutlets was thawing. "Frank's going to live," Sam said. "He's through with playing martyr."

Sam's tone made it clear he would have had some respect for Frank if he'd outright killed himself, but I was stuck on the last-minute sex and what either one of them might have been thinking while he fucked her. I thought of Sharlene in her uniform, the way I'd looked at her the day of my upper GI. I felt like I'd pulled that gun from under my bed and shot her myself.

There was a mystery beyond the old story of loss and anger. "This will settle him down," she might have thought, but I knew it was foolishness to guess at something like that, a kind of secondary rape that made me uneasy with myself.

"He let her fix herself after," Sam said. "She was all buttoned up and such. It was the autopsy that showed us what went on just before. I have to tell you it lowered my opinion of Frank a considerable notch or two."

Like always, Sam didn't speak to the damage a bullet in the head does, and I was thankful for that even though I knew a little about how an exit wound might look in a situation like that. He toed the carpet with his shoe, rubbing it in the way you might scuff out a small ant hill you want to discourage. He watched his foot as if he expected something to move, but it was a carpet in the middle of the living room I never even sat in since Helen had left. "When you were married," he said, "did you ever think Helen was cheating on you?"

"No," I said at once, and Sam nodded like he wanted me to see he'd never thought that about his wife as well.

"What a thing," he said, "thinking another man was inside your wife. It wouldn't sit well."

I thought he was trying to work up an excuse for Frank, that there was justice in what he'd done despite Sam's years of being unfaithful, but then he said, "Imagine if Frank was married to the Virgin Mary. How things would have turned out."

"That wasn't him," I said. "That's over and done with."

"Yes, it is. And so is this."

"He made a choice."

"He fucked up is how I see it," Sam said. "Majorly. He had no claim on her."

I could tell Sam had tried to find something valuable among the mess of this and failed. I didn't blame him. Frank had been a friend, but now he was lost to both of us. The only difference was Sam had tried harder to hold onto something, so maybe that explained what he said next, beginning with "I can't abide this. Absolutely not."

***

I looked it up after Sam left, the thing Sharlene had mentioned about how the soul might be examined. What I found was that in 1907, a doctor named McDougall had put dying patients on a scale, noted their weight to a fraction of an ounce and waited. Joyfully, he measured one less ounce when they were dead, proof, he thought, that the soul had escaped to heaven or hell.

The hardest part for McDougall was waiting. Each time he wished hard for weight loss, and then he began to watch the chest of each dying man, sure this magic flew from the heart. There was a blur, he thought, when the body lightened.

As a control group, McDougall tested dogs, who lost no weight whatsoever, the air around their dying unchanged. I thought of Helen, what she'd make of this story when she read about it in the newspaper. When I couldn't shake it, I called her.

"He's your friend," she said. "It passed through my mind that maybe it was your gun he used on her."

"You liked Sharlene," I said. "I thought you might want to talk."

"OK, Harry," she said, but it sounded like she wanted to hang up until she paused and started again, using a tone I hadn't heard the last few months we'd lived together. "Here's a story that might explain a few things."

She paused again.

"I'm listening," I said.

I heard her exhale, and then she started. "In England, once, there was a mechanic who worked on airplanes, and he found this pin in the lift mechanism that didn't fit quite right. Instead of spending the time to find another pin, he sawed that one off a bit to make it fit better. You know what happened?"

I was sure I knew, but I said "No."

"The plane crashed. Sawing that pin reversed the effect that thing was supposed to have. It made the plane go down."

"I get it," I said, and Helen stayed quiet so long I thought the phone had gone dead.

"Really," she said, as deadpan as a judge.

"Yes," I said, and though I didn't elaborate, I knew she meant for me to understand that the mechanic had committed something worse than sin because he'd ruined other people rather than just himself. That's who hell is for, she was saying. Not for ordinary sin, or else everybody would be there, people like me who made promises to themselves they never kept, the usual kind about bucking up under pressure, being someone who controlled his weaknesses and didn't fall back on alcohol for comfort or excuses.

Right then I wondered if people could ever be happy together. I'd never heard anybody talk about it over drinks. If such a relationship existed, it was something between you and a woman you loved.

* * *

I'd seen Frank once in the three days between that night in his backyard and the murder. He'd walked into my office in the library. "You have time for a beer?" he'd said.

It was just after one o'clock. "At four thirty," I said. "Sure."

He'd nodded like he knew what I'd say. The way he looked around the office made me reconsider the globe I had on a shelf, the drawings of famous old libraries. It was like being a politician with photographs of presidents on the walls. You had to hang old ones up there or else visitors would judge you by the faces you displayed. "You ever get discouraged by all this?" he'd said. "Not being able to keep up with all the books?"

"No."

"What do you think makes people keep writing stuff? There's already more books than the world will ever need and not enough readers for them."

"I hope that's not true," I'd said.

"It's a museum is what it is," Frank said. "I'd go crazy if I had this job." He watched me for a few seconds until I said, "Why's that?"

"It's not what you think," he said. "It's not because I don't read. It's because you're by yourself, and even if somebody's here, there's always silence. Libraries give me the willies. There's not even one of those radios coming out of the ceiling. Christ."

"To each his own," I said, a stupid thing to say.

"Fucking-A it is. I could hit somebody in here. I could smack one of those shushers. Don't you ever want to do that?"

"No," I said, though it was a lie.

"Shhhh. Even when I was a kid, I hated anybody who said 'Shhhh' in school. Who the fuck did they think they were, a goddamn teacher? And I sure as hell hated the teachers that said 'Shhhh.'"

"There's places that need to be quiet," I said.

"Shut the fuck up," Frank said in a way that spoke to the past and the present. He grinned then, the way a boy happy to get away with something would.

Frank's eyes skipped from side to side as if he wanted to see somebody looking at him, one of the men still young enough to fight if he called him out because he disapproved of him talking out loud in a library. In another few seconds, I thought, I'd have to tell him to quiet down and then he'd say, "Sorry, OK," or, "Who says?" or, "Fuck off," deciding which way the afternoon would end.

"When you were growing up, did you ever see a librarian who was a man?" he said, quieter now, nearly a whisper, so I knew he was calming down.

"No," I said.

"I always thought you needed to see what you might be-come," he said. "You notice what's what when you're a kid, and it sticks to you. Nurses are all women; secretaries are all women; your teachers in grade school are all women, what everybody sees like that."

"Not always."

He looked around the room as if he wanted me to see the evidence that only a certain kind of person sat in a library, that there was something about the old men with their newspapers that proved his point so that when he shrugged and left without saying anything else, I'd have something important to remember.

* * *

My story with Helen was as familiar as the road you take to work each morning, the one you barely notice as you weave through traffic and listen to music you would never buy and play inside your house. I hadn't been angry or jealous. I'd said, "Whatever you want," like a man who hadn't loved her for years.

Which made me wonder about Frank, how someone could feel so strongly about someone that he had to destroy her. And himself. Or maybe it wasn't hard at all if your anger rose from such love. What did I know about intensity, the life that follows from it?

He put the gun to his chest when the time came. And he fired, I'll give him that. He blew out a lung and under other circumstances than being attended to immediately, he would have died.

But there they were, the police and the paramedics called in with hope for his wife already dead in the car. So I'm thinking he hadn't the nerve, that he gave himself a chance with where he placed the gun. That he wanted to save face in front of that firepower they had pointed his way.

But Sam Pagala knew better, what with being there, and so did I, just hearing it from him. If Frank wanted to die, all he had to do was point that gun at the police. It didn't take a bullet in his brain or heart, just the thought of it aimed at those uniforms.

And isn't that the issue here? Didn't he want to show them?

It seemed an awful thing to think—that carrying an anger like Frank's might be a good thing in a world where people fall away from each other so easily.

You can't have that, I told myself. Absolutely not. But it took me a long time to shake it, thinking there was a misery inside of getting along with everybody that was just this side of hell.

AFTER ARSON

THE SOFT THUD ABOVE ME might be the cat, but I know it is my son placing the barbells on the carpet. Derek works at the weights in a way that makes me worry it is hopeless. On the first night he tried to lift, he struggled to push just the empty bar over his head.

Now, without walking upstairs to check, I know there are two small doughnuts, two and one half pound each, he presses ten times. He has asked for a bench; he has rummaged through the medicine chest for talcum powder, equating his efforts with the delicate needs of a billiards expert.

These workouts sustain his faith in growth. Only one boy in his class is smaller. Derek understands heredity, and he is frustrated by the disparity between our heights.

I have reminded him about favorable odds and time. He finishes three sets and starts down the steps to check for results in a mirror by the side door. When he sees I am watching, he turns his back to the glass. "No more 'wimp,'" he says. "Or 'beanpole.' I'll ring the bell this summer when the carnival comes to the Rotary field."

I tell him there's a secret to the carnival's test of strength, that the game he's asked me to try three summers in a row is rigged. "The wire that the weight's on is slack," I say. "No matter how hard you swing the hammer, the weight won't rise all the way to the bell."

Derek shakes his head and recounts the number of bells rung by older boys and fathers, unlike me, who are willing to test themselves. "The carnival guy always takes the slack out for a swing or two," I explain. "He makes sure somebody rings the bell occasionally, or else nobody else will play after a while."

Derek thinks for a second. "You're just embarrassed," he finally replies.

* * *

At the end of one of those nights when I return home late, my wife is waiting for me with an expression of crisis stitched onto her face. Liz is otherwise unmarked, so I expect to hear about my mother's heart or splints applied to Derek or one of our other two children.

This time I am wrong. It is Derek, all right, but instead of a doctor, a policeman. What does a boy just turned eleven have to do to be detained for questioning? In a small town like ours, not much, but this is serious, Liz insists, a fire in a public rest room, the near-catastrophic spread of flames through a theater.

Or something close to that. Paper towels had been lit. They had flared, according to what Liz has been told, threatening the brittle wooden walls of the converted barn, but Derek and the theater were still standing. Nevertheless, a confrontation was waiting for me in the theater office, and I was expected to drive back across town to meet it.

Derek claims, Liz says, that he had been only an accidental witness, standing in the rest room when another boy had tried to prove himself with matches. After I ask why I am needed then, Liz shrugs.

When I arrive, Derek is sitting across a table from a policeman who simply nods when I enter. I figure him at once for a tyrant or a fool. "SELINSGROVE SEALS" is printed in white, block letters on the front of the red cap Derek wears. I check off a series of hard-edged possible responses to the stupidity of what I anticipate is about to happen.

"Tell me what happened while your father listens," the policeman says.

There were long pauses in the rehearsal, Derek explains. His part, as well as the other boy's, was small, and they had time to fill. When he watched the other boy light the towels, it had seemed like a performance, something he was expected to watch. He had not even helped throw water when the towel roll opened up across the floor, flames traveling like thick thread. Even when it was over, it still seemed like the other boy's role, and Derek hadn't said anything to anybody because nothing looked to him like it was damaged.

Except, I think, now Derek is accused because he expects everyone to be truthful and doesn't understand the word-against-word dilemma of investigation. I look to the policeman to see how he's interpreting, but instead of saying anything, he nods again and leaves the room.

* * *

Sometimes I am surprised by things. Sometimes there are moments when the world is pliable enough for hope. When the policeman returns, he is pleasant and articulate. Derek is believed. The other boy has lied so badly he could do nothing, eventually, but confess.

"It's because you had a coat and tie on," Liz says when we get home. "Being dressed like that at ten-thirty at night impresses the police." Derek twirls his hat on one finger, blurring the stylized blue seal below the white letters. A couple of revolutions and it flies off into the centerpiece of dried flowers.

"Everything is going soft on this planet," the policeman had said while Derek was retrieving his jacket. "You need to keep a watchdog now just to keep from sinking into the world."

"We have a cat," I had said, and he had looked quizzically at me. He had laughed, too, although a beat was missed.

The hat with the aggressive blue seal displaces the flower arrangement. "He's still in the play," I say. "The other boy is being replaced."

"On such short notice?"

Derek reaches out to pull the hat free. He begins to twirl it again.

"It doesn't take De Niro. Somebody can learn it in a few days."

This time the hat lands by my feet. I pick it up in a way that keeps Derek from asking for it back.

***

At breakfast, before his brother and sister come downstairs, Derek explains the urgency of his recurring dream. It is my fault, Liz reminds me, that he has it.

He is running from the pods. All of us have changed, invaded by aliens. Beginning with the remake we watched more than two years ago and ending with the original last month, Derek has sat through two versions of *Invasion of the Body Snatchers*.

After watching the remake, he'd gone to sleep, as usual, with his Darth Vader punching bag—one of those tall, weighted balloons that sways and bounces and always returns to upright—standing beside his bed. An hour later he'd woken to the certainty of an attack by the pods. A life-size one stood near his face.

"Am I changed?" he had screamed. "Am I changed?"

I had tried to reason with him. I had turned on the light to show him Vader's plastic face.

"You're pretending," he had said. "You're a pod man. The real you is in the garbage."

Vader had to be deflated. A night light had been found in a drawer. "Eight years old," Liz had said, "and you've given him a changeling complex."

The pods have returned several times a year since then, and his horror stories, when I try to extract them, break off in him like ticks. I imagine holding some kind of medicinal flame to each of them. I imagine his watching the original film when he is eleven will show him it is time to stop worrying. Instead, I have to listen to his revelation that everyone who is not real has a tiny red mark behind his ears. After I pour the orange juice, I allow him to check near my hair line.

"Every time," he says, "I am the only one left who isn't changed." When I ask him what he sees behind my ears, he shrugs and returns to his cereal.

***

That night we watch a television show that shows clips of famous televised magic. Near the end a magician makes the Statue of Liberty disappear. The statue weighs 225 tons, we learn, seeing an audience follow the action in person.

The magician prattles on about freedom and immigrants and his mother, an enormous curtain tellingly closed behind him. "I remember this one," I say, "but I didn't watch."

A set of commercials comes on. "He can't do it," Derek says. "It's just a trick."

After the commercials, when the curtain finally opens, the statue is gone. Searchlights play over the empty space; the live audience is astonished. And then the magician closes the curtain again and begins to preach about the importance of freedom, running on so long I tell Derek he's moving the audience, not the statue. "They think they're looking at the same space, but he's turned them," I say. "Now he's stalling while he turns them back."

Derek leans forward and stares. When the statue reappears, he sits up and says, "You're wrong. It's a fake statue. He's changed it just like the body snatchers."

***

"It's him, Dad," Derek says a few weeks later, pointing at the newspaper. I am watching a Pittsburgh Pirate relief pitcher walk the winning run into scoring position.

He places the paper on my lap and shows me the picture on the front page. I glance down at one of those faces you know but don't know. "Who?" I say.

"The policeman at the playhouse."

"Oh." I think of how reflexively I wave at such people, hoping a gesture is enough. A left-hander trudges into the nearly hopeless situation. The heart of the lineup will surely drive in the run that will put the Pirate losing streak at five.

"He got killed. Somebody shot him four times."

"Around here?" For a moment, just before I pick up the newspaper and begin to read, I think of how many times someone has said this, looking around the vulnerable spots in his house as if insulation could keep out every kind of weather.

The killer, the paper says, had been seeking revenge. He had stepped out of the darkness and fired four times through the patrol car window.

It turned out he was mistaken. The policeman he had meant to kill was sitting in another car at the beginning of the speed trap. They had switched cars. It was boring, after all, to do nothing but read numbers. Thirty minutes had passed since the killer had been given a speeding ticket—time enough to go home, load a rifle, and return. Perhaps the road, two lanes along the river, had reminded him of a frontier. There was a Country & Western bar a short distance away. After he fired the shots, the killer walked to it and ordered a beer and smoked a cigarette, according to a patron, by taking cowboy-film drags.

So the arrest had been simple. There was even an eyewitness. Parked in front of the patrol car was a pickup truck whose driver was being cited for littering. Sitting under the dome light, the policeman had been writing the citation when the avenger fired. The litterer had looked out into the face of a man who had just fired a rifle into the body of a policeman. They had stared at each other until the man on foot had crossed the road, tossed the rifle onto the seat of his jeep, and walked off toward the tavern.

Later, everyone in the bar claimed they knew he was the killer because he had been the only one who had not rushed to the door when a man shouted from outside that someone had been shot.

"He didn't take no mess from nobody," a friend explained when he was interviewed. "He didn't allow nothin' to fool with his head."

There were short biographies of both victim and killer. There were comments from teachers and relatives. The killer's friend ran on for half a column. "Bad news went down when you messed with him," he said at the close.

* * *

After a spring of record rain, nothing for over a week but heat, the black flies prosper. In this part of Pennsylvania there is a characteristic fanning of the face in warm weather. A stranger riding through town would wonder at the mannerism. If he stopped to inquire, he would quickly discover its source and either be assimilated or covered by welts.

For fifteen minutes I have been brushing the gnats away and watching the lot in front of the college auditorium fill with police cars. Five hundred uniformed mourners have been promised. An equal number of civilians.

The black flies break into small clouds and cover the crowd. Derek walks across the grass toward me. He looks strange in pants—school has been out for a week. His expression is equally out of place. A first funeral should be some vague great-uncle who seemed to have been born old.

We sit far to the side. There are, perhaps, a dozen people we know here. None of them are policemen. The service is a

Catholic one. Several priests stand on the stage, but only one is elaborately dressed. He will say the important things.

The program, I realize, is exactly like a church service. At least until the homily, which is filled with allegories for hope and faith. Derek looks straight ahead. He may be afraid to turn, believing someone will lecture him immediately about behavior. However, when I don't read the responses or sing the hymns, he is silent, too.

When the policemen who choose to take communion file through the aisles, all of them cup their hands in front of them. Some lessons stay. No one is self-conscious.

An hour of this, prayer and praise. A large picture is mounted above the closed casket. Even from thirty rows back I can tell it's an enlargement of the photograph in the newspaper.

The priest concludes by telling the story of a little girl's fantasy of heaven. She claimed, when asked, that everyone had the same expression of happiness. It was that perfect smile, she said, the one that animals have in my picture books. Derek appears to be listening closely.

And then the five hundred policemen exit. They are forming, I am sure, an elongated corridor of grief through which the coffin and the family will pass.

NEIGHBORS

KEVIN SHIMMEL

KEVIN HAD BEEN UP SINCE the day before, arguing with himself. Inside his house it was dark and then gray and now dark again. Nobody could say his house was abandoned even though Susan, the bitch next door, used words like *shell* and *decrepit* and *ruined*. There was running water. A toilet. A shower if he had a mind to use it. And there was electricity, which counted for something, even if the only lights with working bulbs were in the basement.

Kevin had figured he could sleep during the day, so exhausted it wouldn't matter about the light coming through the windows that had no curtains or drapes. But now it had been nearly forty hours since his last rest, and he'd decided he wasn't going to court, not when he knew how that would end, the judge using that scolding look that shouted "scumbag" or "shithead."

Now it was only about how much time Kevin had before anybody would be looking for his neighbor Susan, and here she was at last, coming up the walk just before midnight, so he had eight hours, plenty of time and no excuses to put off what had to be done. He waited a moment longer, until he saw her enter the row house next door, the one she'd fixed up so much she hated the condition of everybody else's on the block. Then he felt his way down the stairs, turned on the high intensity lights by the workbench, and groped through the hole he'd made by tearing out bricks in the wall between their basements. He wished that judge was here right now so he could show him, in the light that he turned on at the bottom of her stairs, how her side of the house was no different in the basement. But no, that judge wasn't about to come take a look, and Kevin had had enough, suffering through the first two go-rounds in court, decisions that cost him $40,000 in fines, money he'd never had and never would have. If Susan disappeared, that would be the end of it. He read about those cases every week it seemed like, witnesses not showing up, cases being dismissed.

She was above him already, her shoes tapping on the kitchen floor, so much in a hurry like she always was, but she'd find time to come down and turn off the light at the switch at the bottom of the stairs. She'd notice the light under the door because she was like that, sniffing around after everything, and this was the last thing she'd ever notice, the nitpicker, because Kevin was committed to making sure of that with the saw and the tin snips and the plastic bags waiting on his workbench.

ROBERT SHIMMEL

When his son died after he was arrested for allegedly murdering his next door neighbor, the victim's brother had said, "Good. Now I don't have to kill him."

As if somebody who didn't know a thing about it firsthand knew every detail. As if he was God. As if he knew the police had lied when they said Kevin had killed himself while leg-shackled and handcuffed in the back of the police van, making his son out to be some sort of Houdini getting his belt out of his pants and around his neck during the short drive to the police station.

There would be a conspiracy of silence now. Robert could see that coming. What did the police call themselves, the thin blue line? Well, it was thick as hell when it came to his son, and now they had to back each other with that asinine story.

But the woman's brother was the worst of the lot. What was he all about talking like that to the reporters? It was so easy to run his brother-of-the-victim mouth with nobody ever to call him on it.

ALEX HILLYARD

Alex had always admired the Old Testament way of seeing things, and now here it was begging to be used. If Kevin Shimmel's body could be stolen from the morgue, if there was a chance to cut it into pieces and bag them, Alex was ready to finish that eye-for-an-eye operation.

The police had told him about the way it looked inside that asshole's fucked up house. The corroded bathroom, the peeling wallpaper, the floor warped and sagging from water pouring through the holes in the roof. Cat shit and porn magazines everywhere. Gay porn at that, the fucker.

"Who the fuck lives in a place like this?" the first cop inside had told Alex. "But then I saw the blood on the guy, and I stopped giving any sort of shit about the condition of the house."

Karen's daughter was standing on a chair in Karen's old wedding dress when her husband Ray handed her the paper saying, "Don't you know this woman somehow?" and Karen, after taking a look, was afraid she'd faint right then and there, tumbling them all to the floor.

The dress had seemed like the best idea ever. Her daughter was nearly the size Karen had been in 1974 when she'd worn that dress to marry Ray. Now, with her head feeling lopsided, she had to tell RaeLynn to step down because she had to find something before she went to pieces over such news Ray had shoved right under her nose.

"You let me look," she said. "I know right where it is," correct about that, pulling out the photo album from under a dozen others that were up to date, 1998–1999 inked on the cover of the top one.

"Your wedding pictures?" RaeLynn said.

"Leave them out when you're finished."

"Sure, baby," Karen said, but she didn't tell her the murdered woman Ray had pointed to in the paper was right there in the pictures in that album.

KEVIN SHIMMEL

Buy cheap. Fix fast. Rent to people who think gentrification is a synonym for a meaningful life. That's what Kevin had started out to do these past six years, but he'd come up against it when the money he'd borrowed from his father ran out. Now everybody at Wendy's was telling him he'd be there forever like the rest of them because what else had he done since quitting college twice except deliver pizzas.

They didn't believe he'd fixed the other properties, and neither did Susan Hillyard, even when he offered to show her the houses. She'd just said, "You haven't touched this place," like his talking sounded like frogs croaking.

It was all about money, didn't she know that? Nobody had rented the other two places. People who looked at the houses acted like if things weren't perfect inside and out they couldn't move in. Like anything was perfect. Like maybe fixing a few things themselves was too much to ask for. People who owned no fucking tools. People who thought hardware stores stocked supplies for servants.

ROBERT SHIMMEL

The day after the murder, a reporter found Robert standing outside Susan's house. "You someone who knew the killer or the victim?" he said, and Robert stared at the last two sections of the twelve-house row, both houses empty now, and thought about lying in order to learn just how prejudiced this reporter, twenty-five at the oldest, might be.

"I'm Kevin Shimmel's father," he finally said. "Nobody's proved anything yet."

"So you think your son is a victim here, too?"

"I know my son. How gentle he is. An Eagle Scout, did anybody tell you that? He couldn't do this. Not this way like some kind of monster."

"What else do you know?"

"The police murdered him. They lynched him."

The reporter didn't argue. "I know nobody will listen because this is so awful—beating a woman, strangling her, cutting her up. Nobody I ever met could have done this. The house was all boarded up. Some crazy homeless guy did it, and my son just happened to walk in on him."

The reporter glanced at the house and then across the river that ran below the cliff at the end of the street less than a hundred feet away. Robert thought he was choking back a smile, and he felt warm as his hands curled into fists. "I met that woman once," he said. "She lived right next to my son with her piano and her books and enough money to fix up a house bought cheap."

The reporter tapped his pen against his closed notepad. "You know what she said to me, a stranger?" Robert said, his voice rising. "'Your boy should keep his promises.' Like I'd know right away what she was referring to. Like he owed her anything just because she wanted the street as fancy as she was."

The reporter gestured toward the yellow crime tape that sealed off the front door. "No disrespect," he said, "but you think if you went downstairs in there, you might have cause to doubt?"

"You have a son?" Robert said.

"Yes," the reporter said. "Two boys, as a matter of fact, though not full grown like yours. All I'm saying is the circular saw and the high intensity lights the police described might make even a father reconsider."

The heat from Robert's anger rose into this throat. He had to swallow before he said, "You write what you want then, Daddy."

"I want to thank you," is what Alex told the policeman who acknowledged he'd been driving the van with Kevin Shimmel in the back. "I'm Alex, Susan's brother."

"We wanted to kill him too, but we didn't."

"I know you can't admit it, but you're heroes." Alex had asked for him and the other arresting officer by name. He'd waited half an hour for their shift to end, but only this one had come out to greet him.

"There's no heroes in this one," the policeman said, backing through the door as he spoke, keeping eye contact in a way that made Alex uneasy.

"Thank you for trying to be then."

"It's not what you're here for, but I can give you a hypothetical," the policeman said, eyes forward to manage the eight cement steps to the street. In front of the police station, the sidewalk was wet from the shower that had passed while Alex waited inside. The policeman stepped off the curb and stood in the shallow water that ran toward the nearby storm drain.

"I understand," Alex said, but the policeman didn't speak until Alex stepped into the street as well and stood, like the policeman, to face the traffic.

"Hypothetically," the policeman said, "after a while on this job, some police can tell which of the crazies will do themselves if they let them, if they're given a choice."

"How often do you let them?" Alex said, and when the policeman stayed silent, he added, "Hypothetically."

"It has to make us sick," the cop finally said. "We're not monsters."

Two days after the murder, Russell wrote a letter to the editor because he thought people needed to be reminded that Kevin Shimmel, like everyone, was more than just one moment of his life. He'd known Kevin Shimmel, which was more than all the other people who'd spewed their anger across the newspaper's editorial pages could claim. Those people concentrated on the cat shit in the house, the gay S and M porn, and the stories about how Kevin Shimmel had been in more than one psychiatric facility.

So he'd written his own letter, a long one, reminding people that Kevin had said his house had been firebombed, that there was more to account for disrepair than neglect. And when people, himself among them, had ridiculed Kevin at the neighborhood association meeting, telling him to stop coming until he did something besides make up stories, that cold shoulder might have been a last straw for a man working against the odds to make something of himself.

And what harm could it do, at the conclusion of his letter, to suggest that the people in his neighborhood should ask for their own forgiveness as they said a prayer for Susan Hillyard? And a prayer for Kevin Shimmel, too.

KAREN VOSS

The newspaper report let everybody understand that the girl Karen had known years ago, her young neighbor that summer she'd married Ray, had been found in five pieces, two legs, two arms, and a torso. The police had interrupted the killer or he would have taken off her head. Was that some comfort to her family? And were there photographs that would inevitably be leaked?

When Karen opened her album of wedding pictures, she began at the back, where the reception photos were. Next to last were two photos of the best man and the next-door neighbors' children decorating the car she and Ray would drive to Lake Erie for their brief, four-day honeymoon. In one, the girl, Susan, is helping to string flowers across the roof. In the other, she's looping crepe paper through door handles, the "Just Married" sign already taped to the back window.

Alex, the boy, looked to be about ten, a year or two younger than Susan, just as excited as his sister. Twenty-five years, that girl had left, and Karen, sitting there while her daughter said, "What, Mom? What?" felt like some fortune teller cursed with actually knowing what would happen to people, seeing their cancers and heart attacks and violent deaths.

ALEX HILLYARD

Susan had been talking everybody into a park and a promenade. Like she lived in some part of town where people had nothing to do but go for walks and play with their kids. On the other side of the street there weren't any facing houses because the level land narrowed near a cliff that overlooked the river. She insisted a park could be put there because the strip of vacant land ran for a hundred yards past where the next street dead-ended until it disappeared where a cul-de-sac had been constructed right to the cliff's edge, a guardrail provided just in case. It would take a fence along the edge, for sure, something to reassure parents of small children, but the cliff was there anyway, unprotected now, so no one would object.

That was his sister. Working through things. Considering all sides ahead of time so by the moment somebody wanted to argue, she'd already addressed whatever they objected to. And all that smartness and get-up-and-go in Susan's head had been about to be sawed off and dumped.

Her arms and legs were already bagged. That's what he knew. He found a photo of his sister from the waist up and placed his thumbs over her arms and stared at what was left of her. Torso was the word they used in the newspaper. Her terribly savaged corpse.

KAREN VOSS

Two more photos forward in Karen's wedding album and there was the picture of young women and girls reaching for the bouquet she'd tossed. Her parents' house had been under repair. That was in the photo, too. The back side of the house had the siding stripped, some sort of heavy paper with the company's logo covering the wall.

It had been a hot day, and though her father had promised nobody would see the back of the house, guests went out the rear door "for air," and after a while, the crowd was so large behind the house that she had to step onto the back porch to toss the bouquet. Nobody mentioned the stripped siding and the thick, brown paper. It was only when the photos came back that she was ashamed of the back of the house.

Just as she'd thought, Susan was in the photograph, her young, lean body actually off the ground a few inches, hands outstretched, reaching for the bouquet with a dozen of Karen's old sorority sisters. Now all Karen could think of as her daughter said she was ready to climb back up on the chair, was the way people hung themselves, kicking the chair out from under themselves and strangling. "No," she said. "Just stand there. I'll finish it this way," and she knelt on the linoleum floor.

"What's wrong, Mom?" her daughter said, but Karen slipped a half dozen straight pins between her lips, using just enough pressure to keep them from skidding down her throat or onto the floor. It's what anyone would do, Karen thought, if she wanted her hands free as she did the work from her knees.

ALEX HILLYARD

The organ recital Alex had agreed to attend with Susan was Sunday evening. "If I'm taking you out to dinner," she'd said, "the recital is part of the package."

"It's organ music on a Sunday," he said as she drove them from the restaurant to the church. "Are we going to have to sing?"

"He's not playing hymns," Susan told him.

"I'm joking."

"Sure you are."

The church was enormous, room in the pews, he guessed, for five hundred. The recital, the program declared, was called "Getting Down with the B-Boyz."

"Does he think his audience is from the hood?"

"It's for publicity," Susan said. "And it works. There was an article in the paper this morning. The title got somebody curious. And just look at how it's filling up."

The church looked to be more than half full. Three hundred people to listen to an organist, Alex marveled, but he had no idea how many would have stayed home if the recital had been called "Classical Organ Music."

"I have to testify in the morning," Susan said just before the overhead lights dimmed and the lights above the chancel went up. "This at least takes my mind off it for an hour and a half."

Alex turned and looked at her, lowering his voice. "That guy is a major douche bag."

"I'd buy his place if I had the money to fix it up just to get rid of him and get a roof over it."

"He's never going to touch it."

There was a ripple of applause as the performer crossed the chancel and slid onto a seat behind the organ. "My friend Alicia says I should get a restraining order," Susan said.

"Those things are useless."

"They're a warning, at least. There are consequences."

"So you think you need one?"

The crowd settled. "Maybe," Susan whispered," and the recital began.

ROBERT SHIMMEL

Such a blizzard of loss, Robert thought, surprised by the expression surfacing in his mind, then reminding himself he'd been reading the magazines his wife subscribed to, keeping himself occupied and trying to learn something about her he didn't already know. His son was dead, accused of murder. He'd lived in his house for twenty years, and Robert, during every one of those years, would have bet his own life on the impossibility of Kevin committing murder. What was his wife, struggling with simply walking, capable of? What was she thinking, during their thirty years together, that he couldn't imagine?

What he was remembering now was how the snow swirled through the holes in the roof as his son walked him through the second floor of the house he'd bought dirt cheap. "You can get rich doing this," he'd said, though by then both of them were surely thinking of the other unrented properties while they shivered in the February cold. He'd stared up at the sky. The wind made sounds through the open spaces; clouds scudded by and blue appeared, yet the snow still swirled. His son, then, had looked up and seen. Both of them had smiled. "You'll see," Kevin had said. "Just you wait."

Robert had long ago known he'd never get back the money he'd loaned to Kevin, but not repaying a debt didn't make his son evil. Plenty of people have investments that jump the tracks. The only thing that made his son different was he wouldn't let go of an idea anybody else could see had come to nothing.

You could make a case for the goodness of that attitude, working the big rock of it up a steep hill like the guy in one of those old myth stories his wife would tell him when she needed an example. Always with the stories, his wife. Instead of just saying "hopeless," she would start in with the word *like*. If that's what comes of reading all the time, he wasn't missing anything.

This was something to say straight out: His son was a fuck-up, not a killer. Nobody had proved anything. Those cops had rehearsed their story. Anybody could see that. No fucking way it would stand up, but who would ever take the case, and what could he do about it when his wife promised him she would leave if he ever pursued it, dragging them through the muck for nothing because nobody would ever change their minds about this. Nobody. Not ever.

KAREN VOSS

The monster, when Karen saw his photograph in the Wednesday morning newspaper, looked older than the twenty-seven the paper said he was, with the sort of scraggly beard a man wore out of neglect rather than style. She tried to discover something unnatural and predatory in his eyes, but there was nothing but ordinary, and she felt herself grow chilled.

When she examined the victim's photo, the paper reprinting the one it had used the day before, she felt she was checking for the accuracy of a computer-generated "how she would look now" photo because, even though Susan had lived next door, Karen had been busy with high school and college, and all she had to rely on were the three glimpses of her from the wedding album.

She scanned Susan's face, finding details in the nose and mouth that made her say, "Yes," and then, for a long moment, made her think of destroying the wedding dress, afraid that RaeLynn would someday have the need to examine her wedding photos to verify the victim of something unimaginable.

"That's your mother-of-the-bride hormones taking you on a wrong turn," her husband said when she told him about her fear. "It's a coincidence. Somebody's old neighbor gets killed every day," and she gave him a look that stopped him from explaining further. She didn't tell him that she thought of contacting the boy, whose name, the newspaper had said, was Alex.

ALEX HILLYARD

Fuck's sake, did the asshole who wrote the letter think nobody in Susan's family read the newspaper? *We should ask forgiveness for treating our neighbor badly. It's not too much to end by saying a prayer for Kevin as well as Susan.*

Some jackass liberal. They're like that in the neighborhoods around universities, so it wasn't a surprise, but this time it was his sister, and forgiveness wasn't up for discussion. It was the same voice that squawked about reparations to blacks or Indians for things that happened 150 years ago. They loved picking out the lame to coddle, the runts of the litter. The Jimmy Carter type, admitting to lusting in his heart as if that wasn't common to everybody over the age of twelve.

The self-righteousness of it all. To say it out loud in the same newspaper where his sister's story had been told and retold for nearly a week. What else could he make of it but as a way for the guy to feel better about his own self? And when he checked on where this guy lived, it didn't surprise Alex one bit that he worked at the university where everybody could make themselves feel better by studying the misery of others and suggesting compassion, jerking themselves off to the pornography of sanctimony.

Ordinarily, being approached by a stranger coming right up the back steps to the porch would be alarming, but the man, Russell noticed at once, was wearing a dark suit, a white shirt, and gray tie. He looked like a funeral director in that outfit, and that's what put Russell off his guard.

"Forgive this," the man said, skidding two photographs across the glass-topped table to where Russell sat. He found out later that the picture of the torso the man showed him wasn't the dead woman at all, that the legless, armless body belonged to a woman murdered ten years before, the photo used in a crime magazine long out of business. But side by side with a photo of the woman he'd known, it was convincing, and he'd looked quickly from the photos to the man, so nearly any woman's body would have done the trick.

Russell's son had come outside, thirteen and curious, looking down at the pictures before he could turn them over. "Your father is a stupid cunt," the man in the suit said, and Russell sucked his breath in at his son's expression.

And then, when Russell picked up the pictures, standing to say, "I'm sorry, but these need to leave with you," the man punched him once in the stomach, a blow that took the air out of him in such a way he couldn't speak, the pictures fluttering to the floor.

His son knelt to pick them up. He looked at each one again and handed them to the man in the dark suit. "Write a letter to the editor about that," the man said as Russell began to straighten. "Use my name, Alex Hillyard, and ask for forgiveness for making me punch you. You fuck."

Somebody at the neighborhood improvement meeting asked him if he'd been in Desert Storm, the tone all wrong, nothing in it about service and sacrifice and personal history. The guy meant he acted fucked up somehow. Jittery. Intense. Meandering.

There it was—his father's word. "You're meandering instead of following the straight path," he always said, as if life took place in a narrow canyon you entered and had to follow unless you wanted to waste forever going back and starting over like somebody just out of prison.

Kevin had been speaking up about improvements. He had ideas—bricked crosswalks, a wrought iron fence, antique lamps, cherry trees, benches. Some people clapped, but mostly they seemed to be looking him over, and afterward, that guy asked his question before Kevin saw Susan, the piano player he'd met a few weeks earlier walking toward him. "They've heard nearly all of that already," she said. "Except for the antique lamps. That's new." She had the same impatient expression on her face she'd worn when they'd met, coming out of the house next to his and saying, "The roof is where you should begin."

As if that was a way of introducing herself. As if she was absolutely sure he'd fuck it up.

KAREN VOSS

Since her wedding, Karen had lived twenty-five uneventful years until she read about the murder five days before her daughter's wedding. She had only the one child, but she hadn't lost any to miscarriage or accident. Her husband was faithful and reliable. They lived in a house with only four years left on a mortgage, and she worked part-time in a coffee shop as much out of needing something to do as to put aside extra money for restaurants and vacations. This murder, though, was the end of ordinary. Evil had slipped into her life.

At her daughter's wedding she counted the girls who looked to be within a year or so of twelve. Three of them, all excited. It was crazy to imagine her old wedding dress was an omen for girls she barely recognized. Karen would be an old woman in twenty-five years, past seventy. "What's your name?" she asked each one, but she didn't write the names down. She wasn't crazy. She was just being a good host, the mother of the bride.

ROBERT SHIMMEL

His boy had been raised along the fairways of a golf course, the wide swath of green the color of Christmas wrapping paper. His boy had steady customers for his business selling fifty-cent golf balls to men and women who knew they'd been found in the deep rough or among the thick pines. Five summers, from age six to ten, he'd sold to men and women who, laughing, sometimes recognized a ball they'd lost, one marked with some simple design of dots or their initials because more than half of them used Titleists.

Although Robert had set aside a used set of clubs in the basement, saying, "For you, Kevin, when you're ready," his boy had never learned the game. The summer Kevin turned eleven they moved to a house with one floor, his wife struggling with arthritis in her knees, the house six miles from that course, the neighborhood full of old married couples who paid Kevin to mow lawns and tend shrubbery between breaks of television and video games.

His boy was a businessman. College made him impatient, all three of those colleges in three different states, one semester each. There was money to be made in housing, he'd said. Near a large university a landlord can become rich; that's what he'd learned from enrolling. All the boy needed was a stake, and with his wife not wanting to travel, using a cane by then, lost in books and magazines, what better way to spend his money, giving his boy a start?

RUSSELL REEVES

A house is personal, Russell understood that. All along, he'd been on Susan's side, encouraging her, because everyone's investments needed to be protected. That was fundamental. A man who exposed his neighbor's possessions to ruin from rain was invading her home like a thief.

That's all he admitted to, a one-sided way of seeing the dispute. Him and everybody else in the neighborhood, rightfully so. But there was arrogance to avoid. Condescension. Contempt. Name-calling and belligerence. If her brother could have been talked down, if he had stayed and sat with him, the photos swept aside, Russell would have shared stories about Susan.

In his living room, Susan had played the piano that he'd bought for his daughter, Ashley. She'd given Ashley lessons for more than a year when, one afternoon, as the lesson ended, she began to play. He didn't know the name of the song or the composer, and there was no music in front of her. A marvel, he'd thought. Though he knew there were many people who could do this, no one had ever performed like that in his house.

The music went on for three or four minutes, no longer, and Russell had risen to his feet in the adjoining room and positioned himself so he could see Susan through the doorway. She was striking the way she sat so upright, her hands and fingers moving rapidly. Russell had felt a stirring of desire.

Susan's fingers touched each key perfectly. No, beyond perfect, because it wasn't a question of being correct, it was a question of touch, the possibilities of pressure through the fingertips. For those few minutes, Russell believed that an accomplished pianist would make an extraordinary lover.

He wouldn't have told her brother that, of course, but he would have told him this: When Susan stopped playing, she'd hugged Ashley and kissed her forehead, and his daughter, thirteen and a year into a desire for independence that was turning toward defiance, softened and held her hand like a child as they walked to the outside door. A brief spell, but a spell nonetheless, and Russell would never forget it, even after his daughter, three months later, announced she knew she would never be any good and wanted to quit.

If Susan's brother had listened, Russell would have told him he was just taking the other side for a few paragraphs. Reminding readers about feelings that seep into what seemed to be a waterproof conscience. After all, Russell had known the killer when he was eager to improve the neighborhood, when he pursued development grants and began to work on his house like anyone would. Who knew that work would last so briefly?

Russell felt like the judge who had to acknowledge an insanity defense for a terrible crime. There was courage in writing his letter to the editor. He was willing to be the spokesperson for generosity and consideration, for the Christian way. And now to be faulted for that? To be loathed?

KAREN VOSS

Her daughter looked beautiful as she danced with a man who looked impossibly young to be marrying anyone. The dress seemed so timeless that Karen thought it could be worn again. "RaeLynn will save the dress, won't she?" Karen said, touching her husband's hand, which was wrapped around a glass of beer a waiter had just poured. "She'll alter it for her own daughter someday."

Ray toyed with the glass, the foam collar sloshing over the lip. "By then," he said, "if that's what you're thinking, everybody will know nothing bad had happened to anybody."

"You don't know that," Karen said.

"It's superstition," Ray said. "A dress can't bring bad luck any more than it can conjure up good."

"Maybe it's just selfishness then," she said.

"The two of us get memories," Ray said. "RaeLynn gets hope and joy."

Kevin had nudged shards of glass off the walk with his heavy, insulated boots. The boots, he remembered, had made him look serious about getting to work. They were scarred and scuffed, and he was sure they had steel toes. You could kick the stuffing out of somebody with boots like that. Or walk with confidence where bent, rusted nails and splintered wood were scattered.

Kevin chattered on about how the weather breaking felt like a friendly shove in the back. "Like the boss is saying now's the time," Kevin had said, raising his eyes briefly toward the sky before refocusing on him. With his boot, Kevin worked three pieces of broken glass into a row and smiled.

"Spring does that," he'd answered, but the holes were still in the roof, and a month later, the few scraggly daffodils wilted, the lone overgrown forsythia gone from golden to green, the house hadn't changed. The pieces of glass Kevin had lined up were still in a row. Kevin, if he'd been back, had managed to improve nothing. It was all he could do not to gather that glass and a hundred other shards, creating the slightest sign of renovation.

KEVIN SHIMMEL

Kevin expected the cop to have his gun drawn when he came up from investigating in the basement, but his hands were empty. "Cuff him" was all he said to his partner.

Kevin saw the cop look at the S and M magazines that were scattered by the couch, his eyes lingering an extra second or two before he stepped around cat shit so dry it would have powdered under his boot.

"Go look," the cop said to his partner, and Kevin listened to the stairs groan under the man's weight. "You goddamned fuck," the cop who'd gone down first said. "Just you wait."

KAREN VOSS

Karen said nothing about the girls at her daughter's wedding to anybody. She might as well expect the Rapture in twenty-five years or whatever else people anticipated, like kids who thought monsters were under the bed. She'd shake it off as soon as her daughter was out of that dress, when her life went back to normal, watching rented movies with Ray, alternating picks so neither of them was ever more than a day away from something they wanted to see.

ALEX HILLYARD

Alex was outside, a block from his sister's house. A week now since he'd done it, slammed that fat do-gooder, and for a moment he wished he was capable of more.

Though it was a Saturday afternoon, the weather nice, none of his sister's neighbors were outside. Some of them, he knew, had children, and yet the street was deserted.

His sister's house would be put up for sale, but the real estate agent wasn't hopeful. The incident, as she called it, was a considerable drawback. And there was still the ruin next door.

He was certain that the neighbors thought of their own property values, and he wondered whether it terrified them that such selfish thoughts came so readily and frequently to them.

Directly below Alex was a heavily traveled four-lane highway, but if he stood back a few steps, the view was nothing but the river and the landscape of the opposite shore, a tree-lined, revitalized neighborhood that swept down to a strip of shoreline restaurants and shops. If there was a bench, even one near the edge, someone could sit and see only a view that people envy.

Alex walked into the patch of sumac and scrub maple trees. He recognized poison ivy, what, his sister had once told him, did as much to keep kids out of danger as their parents' warnings about strangers and long drops from the cliff.

For a while Alex believed that his rage had been sustained by his love for his sister, but now, two weeks after her death, he understood that it was driven by selfishness. As long as Kevin Shimmel had been killed by the police, he could fantasize his own acts of revenge because they would never be tested. "Now I don't have to kill him"—the sentence, by now, felt so much like bragging, he was ashamed, but taking the air out of that smug balloon on his own porch had been so exhilarating that he wished there were other, small revenges to manage.

The park was inevitable. With enough parents of small children, there would be pressure to erect a fence and clear out anything that would encourage what his sister had always called "lurkers." There would be a plaque, Alex was sure of that, too. Susan's name and a sentence or phrase that memorialized her with praise and empathy. He saw where it would go, set into a stone pedestal that would draw visitors to read it. *Graceful, talented, determined*—the words began to come to him. *Beautiful, spirited, independent*—he allowed them to accumulate. He was never coming back here, so Alex could imagine Susan's face on the plaque as well, an entire paragraph of sentiment, visitors astonished by her story for so many years she would outlive him.

ALL SQUARE

DURING MY JUNIOR YEAR IN high school, a month after my mother moved in with a man named Jim Allison, my father, who taught social studies to seniors, was fired. He'd beaten a student. Had found him out and taken him into a faculty bathroom and punched him a dozen times. "I want a word with you" was what my father had said to the boy, and he'd locked the door behind him. He didn't know the boy. Later, he would say if he'd known him he wouldn't have beaten him. "He was a stranger," my father explained. "Knowing a boy would keep me from that."

The boy had punched another teacher. A woman. He'd said, "I hope you have a baby in there," laying his fist into her stomach.

"Unacceptable," my father said. "Absolutely." He'd been working at that school for twenty-four years and had never touched another student, but the superintendent said he had no choice. The boy's family agreed not to press charges if my father was fired. The boy, whose name was Jessie Grant, was suspended for ten days, the longest the school could keep someone away without providing home tutoring, and he agreed to go to anger management sessions. The woman wasn't pregnant, but she called in sick the following day and didn't come back for any one of those ten days the boy was gone.

The teacher's union filed a grievance, but my father didn't protest. "When you see the terribly wrong," he told me, "it's not about choosing. You act or you're with the other team."

My father had played semipro football until I was born and was fond of sports analogies. I took this one to mean he thought the other team had a full lineup, and I couldn't disagree. "I don't count myself special," he went on, but I had to attend that school every day for another year and two months.

For two days no one said anything about my father to me at school. It was like the year before when Joel Eberly had chemotherapy, and he walked around for a week by himself. When a teacher finally called on him, I was surprised Joel's voice sounded the same as it had before his treatments.

On the third day, before home room, two women teachers I'd never had for class paused beside my locker as I pulled out my morning books. "We want you to know we appreciate your father," the younger one said.

I knew her name was Miss Scott and that she taught Spanish. "OK," I said.

The other one, whose name I didn't know, glanced into my locker as if she expected to get to know me better by looking at my books. "You're a junior here, aren't you?" she said.

"Yes," I said, and I closed the door.

"You keep your head up," Miss Scott said. I shifted the books to my right hand and waited. "There's no shame," she added, and both of them turned away.

When I opened my locker before lunch, there was a note stuck in the door. "Your father is a piece of shit," it said, and I wondered, balling it up in my hand, whether it had been written by a student or a teacher. When I walked into the cafeteria,

Mike Fernald waved me over to my regular table. "What's up?" he said, as if I'd been absent for two days.

* * *

The next Sunday my mother called. "I wasn't sure you'd be home," she said. "I thought your father might be making you a churchgoer now, but I at least was sure he'd be in that pew of his."

"Third row, aisle seat," I said. "I went with him last Sunday because of all the trouble."

"I'm sorry for you," she said. "You keep that to yourself, though."

"OK."

"We're both of us fools," she said. "Ed might think he's walking a different path, but they both end up at the same place."

"He doesn't talk about you, Mom. Honest."

"Yes, he does, Jeff. He comes through your front door talking."

"He hardly talks at all." It sounded like a confession, like I wished for her and her drinking to be back in the house because it needed another voice.

"You'll learn, Jeff. After a while, you won't be able to hear yourself think for all the talking he does with his body."

I looked at the clock that sat on top of the closet where the good dishes and silverware were displayed as if they were for sale. I'd given my mother that clock for Christmas the year before, and right then it said 11:18, so I knew my father was listening to a sermon while I waited for my mother to finish.

* * *

My father took a job at the anchor store at the mall. He sold gardening equipment and supplies—lawnmowers, hedge clippers, Weedwhackers. Selling those was easy, my father explained. Customers either bought the good stock or they scraped by with the low-end.

It was fertilizers and weed killers and bags of mysterious nutrients that were problems. People wanted to know what to expect from using these things, and all my father could say was what was already written on the box or bag. The store sold six kinds of grass seed, for instance—did one kind really do better in full sun? And all those ground covers and perennials to be expert about—partial sun, full sun, full shade; acidic soil, alkaline soil. He'd never done anything but cut grass every Saturday morning from April to October and trim the hedges three times a summer, an all-day job with his handheld shears. He'd never even held electric garden tools. "It's not much different than teaching," he said. "You talk with assurance, and people will believe you."

The larger problem for him was people he knew coming into the store. Or worse, students with their parents, teenagers being dragged away from the CD or DVD racks to where their fathers were helping to pick out plants for overdue Easter presents or early Mother's Day gifts. "Those boys look like they're holding cigarettes behind their backs when they see me," he said. "They act like I've just opened the boys' room door."

* * *

My father and I began feeling our way into household tasks. It was easier than I imagined to believe we were doing well at keeping house, mostly because my mother had done such a lousy job. I knew to separate whites from all the dark colors for laundry because I'd been carrying the baskets for years. I knew where the dishwasher detergent was and how to iron shirts because they were already my jobs.

My father had taken to cleaning and dusting and making sure, as he put it, everything was shipshape. I thought he was pleased with his work, that he understood the house looked better now that my mother was gone. He ran the vacuum every other day. "We should paint the living room," he said three weeks after he'd been fired, and he pointed out small scuff marks near the baseboards, a few smudges by the light switches, and a series of dark smears where chairs had been scraped along one wall.

He said that after a month he could get an employee discount at the department store where he worked. He had hours of extra time each night. He didn't have any tests to correct, and it seemed like I was becoming a boy who didn't need much talking to. "Your mother was always upset about something," he said. "It slowed things down. Here we are getting right after everything."

I'd just finished ironing two weeks' worth of dress shirts for him, and he examined the shirts on their hangers, the collars and the sleeves, and then the fronts of each. I thought of him standing among two dozen lawnmowers in those shirts, his employee name tag clipped to a perfectly pressed pocket.

"Fine," he said. "These are fine."

He spread them apart in the closet as if wrinkles would set in them if they touched. "Christine never got the hang of ironing," he said. "She had a mind to send all my shirts and trousers out, but that didn't cut it."

"I'm OK with it, Dad," I said.

"Yes, we are," he said. "We're going to be fine."

* * *

A week later, a Saturday morning, he woke me early and told me to get in the car. I thought we were going for paint because the month was up, but he drove fifteen miles to the town where he'd grown up, the part where there were streets of houses that bordered the overpass for the thruway that looped around our town because somebody had figured 3a way to get a big chunk of it named as a historical district.

We'd driven past his old house fifty times, but I'd never been down the side streets that dead-ended into abandoned buildings where the highway had gone through. "I wanted you to see where I played football for Coach Kravick," he said, parking the car in a patch of knee-high grass. A few steps away, nearly under the overpass, the field my father played his home games on was still there—level and hard-packed and nearly entirely without grass. "Nobody cared much about making the grass grow," my father said. "I don't know if anybody still plays here, but it looks as if they do."

I stopped and got out, thinking my father would follow, but he stayed in the car. I walked toward the field, listening for the click of the car door latch, and when I didn't hear it, I made myself keep walking as if it was important for me to step onto that field.

The field, even in early May, was hard under my feet, the muddy patches shallow depressions in the unyielding surface. I looked up at the thruway, which appeared to be more weathered than I expected something like that to be when it was just eight years old. After I made it to the far sideline, I saw chunks of concrete, broken brick, and pieces of scrap metal lying in a patch of last year's thistle and milkweed. A gust of wind fluttered the sports section of a newspaper up against my ankles, and it looked so old I expected to see headlines about Bill Buckner's World Series error, something Coach Kravick would have used to motivate my father during his last season, telling him about playing through adversity. It was a mistake for my father to come here, I thought. It was like a high school reunion gone bad—classmates changing into older and uglier versions of who my father remembered. "Even with that road up there now, it's the same," my father said when I got back to the car. "It was always like playing at the ass end of everything."

"It looks like a place a visiting team would hate to come to," I said.

My father smiled, and I thought I'd said something that would make a difference in the day. "If you'd played football, you'd know something about looking out for yourself," my father said then, and it sounded like I'd never spoken.

I kept my eyes on the field. "I'm OK, Dad," I said. I wanted my father to understand I wasn't afraid at school, but he was staring through the side window in a way that told me there weren't any words he wanted to hear.

"I'm talking about consequences," he said. "When they're all around you, there's something other than thinking that's called for."

He drove three blocks and parked again, but this time he left the motor running. Across the street was a bar called Tomko's.

"What's up?" I said. There were crime scene ribbons stretched across the front door.

"Coach Kravick got himself killed in there last night," my father said. "Drinking and money."

My father's last game had been seventeen years ago. I looked carefully at the small windows and the huge beer-advertisement banners. I wanted to get out and look around back, but unless my father opened his door, I couldn't move.

"Fats Kravick," he said. "He'd made a bet, and he had words with a man about not paying. Fats slapped the man, and that man went home, got a gun, came back, and killed him right there in Tomko's." My father stared at the door as if he expected to see Fats Kravick walk out with his arm over the shoulders of an old teammate. "A baseball bet," he said. "And here it is barely May."

I looked up at the thruway again, remembering that my father had told me traffic backed up for ten miles during rush hour because the main highway narrowed and ran through that town until I was eight years old. "Fats Kravick was a man you listened to," my father said, and then he added, "I think drinking must be something that closes your eyes in a fight."

I waited for him to go on, but I knew he meant me to remember my first boxing lesson, how I'd shut my eyes as his fists jabbed at me, and he stopped to tell me he already knew I wouldn't hit back. He flicked his fists near my face, telling me to keep my eyes open because anybody else would see his advantage with me and wade in to hurt me. "Your mother has her eyes closed," he said, and for a few seconds I fixed on that yellow ribbon. "You know," he said at last, "I've never allowed myself to take a drink because I was afraid I wouldn't be able to stop."

I'd had a few beers during my sophomore year, and lately I'd been drunk on most Saturday nights. I never thought about drinking on Monday or Tuesday. Drinking was like going to a football game. It was something to do for three or four hours because it was fun.

"When your mother calls," he asked me, "does she tell you about Jim Allison?"

"She doesn't call, Dad," I said, which was true in so far as I meant regularly. And she'd never mentioned Jim Allison.

"I wouldn't use my fists on your mother's new man. She asked for her mess. It's not my doing." My father nosed the car forward, swinging out in a way that nearly pointed us toward Tomko's. "I've seen this Jim Allison," he said, letting the car drift into the oncoming lane before he finally turned the wheel and brought us back. I thought he was going to say more, but he stopped, and I understood that he'd described Jim Allison in that one sentence, that he believed I knew everything I needed to know.

* * *

Jessie Grant talked to me only once after he came back to school. His voice came from behind me as I walked down the hall alone to American history. "You ever worry about what you can't see coming?" he said.

I didn't turn around. There were only three more rooms until the one where my class was held. "That's it," he said, "keep looking straight ahead. That way you won't see anything."

I thought this was how something important happened. Jessie Grant wasn't much bigger than I was, and even though I'd closed my eyes that first night and most of the second, my father had spent three more evenings since he'd been fired showing me the fundamentals of fighting because, he'd said, "He owed it to me now."

I'd told him to forget about it, and each time he had to provoke me into taking a swing at him, punches that wouldn't hurt my mother because I was always backing up as I swung. I was going to be a boy who took his anger and fear into his room, he said. It was like being a masturbator, somebody who's afraid of what he really wants, words that came back to me in the hall.

I knew I should stop, turn, and say something to Jessie Grant, like "What's your problem?" but I kept walking. I heard a second voice say, "He's a pussy," and I tried to gauge how big Jessie's friend was, whether he was so large he'd come along to give me a beating. When I stepped into my history class it was all I could do not to pull the door shut behind me.

Right away, Mike Fernald said, "Jessie Grant's the pussy," at lunch, so I knew he'd seen how I'd been followed. There were three other boys at the table, and all of them nodded or mumbled, "Yeah."

I didn't have to answer. I scooped up some macaroni and cheese with my fork and shoved it in my mouth. "A fucking pussy," Mike said, and that was the last my friends talked about it. For me, May had become a slow countdown to the three months before I had to come back again in the fall. But now that my father was settled into his new job, his situation seemed less necessary and right. True, I still believed the events had come to him without his asking, but I was thankful that the talk in school had turned to the approach of summer.

For my father, with nothing to do to prepare for his job and keeping the house clean simple and quick, it was a time to landscape. It was something he could do alone. He was already learning the nuances of soil additions and the varying degrees of shade. The light lasted in the early evenings now, and he brought home dozens of plants, measuring the spaces between the holes he dug, dragging bags of peat moss and fertilizers from hole to hole. Within two weeks he had a bank of azaleas and rhododendrons; he had a spread of holly and sedum, a patch of peonies and a swath of six kinds of grasses, all of them some other color than green.

Afterwards, he put a sharp edge to where the lawn ended, and then he drilled small holes in the lawn and sprinkled something off-white that I took for weed-killer. When a truckload of mulch arrived, dumped on the side of the driveway where my mother had parked her car, my father immediately took a shovel to it. Except for an hour off for church, he spent a weekend laying it, waving me off as if the outside of our house was his personal responsibility.

That Sunday night, a week before Memorial Day, I watched him walk around the yard. Occasionally he'd bend down and tug at something, but for the most part he looked to be gauging the arrangement of plants, the way you step back from pictures hung on walls to see they're level and aligned with the ones beside them.

I thought it was too late for that. No one would uproot a plant to move it three inches. I thought about going outside and telling him how great the yard looked, but he never once glanced up at the windows as if he expected to see me standing in one, so I watched until I saw him disappear around the side of the house, and then I turned on the television where a baseball game was in the second inning.

***

Monday afternoon I saw my mother in the grocery store near my school. "Hi there," she said. "How are you getting along?" She sounded so cheerful I thought she'd already been drinking in the middle of the afternoon. She was empty-handed, but there was a man leaning on a grocery cart half way up the aisle.

"I'm fine," I said.

She glanced back at the man who I figured for being Jim Allison and took one step closer. "I would love your father," she nearly whispered, "if I could live with him."

Jim Allison had taken two bags of tortilla chips off the shelf, holding them while he examined varieties of salsa. In the cart were three bags of popcorn already popped and two chunks of what looked to be cheddar cheese. My mother followed my eyes to Jim Allison, who lurched a little and caught himself on the cart. "Your father thinks the world is a place for proving you're never wrong," she said. I didn't answer. Nothing made of words seemed like something to use. "Some men set themselves up where it's hard to get to," she added, talking like a teacher—as if I needed to hear everything twice in different words.

I looked at Jim Allison, imagining a man who looked forward to drinking each day like it was the same as watching a baseball team on television. I thought he was a man who would duck when I swung my fist at him, and then stay ducked, crouched, and trying to cover himself. Six days a week was what my mother's schedule had been the last few years she lived with us, taking off Mondays like a restaurant. Coming home from school on Monday had always been awkward, seeing her impatient and edgy as if the late afternoon had settled in like humidity. She'd worked up projects to keep busy, but usually they came down to taking me to a movie at seven o'clock, and then another one at nine, moving directly into the ticket line returning to the dark. "The second movie's always better," she would tell me. "As soon as we're settled, I know I'm not going to cheat because it's always near midnight when we get out."

I thought it was a flawed plan. The bars were still open. If I didn't come along, I was sure she'd park and walk right in. "If I was sick, I would," she said once, when I brought it up, "but I'm not. I can take a day of rest as regular as God."

With my father in the house, my mother seemed desperate; with Jim Allison, she seemed pathetic, someone who needed sense pounded into her. I thought of my father coming upon my mother and Jim Allison in that store, yet keeping his hands to himself and pushing his cart up a different aisle, and I imagined taking one of those salsa jars in my hand and roundhousing it into Jim Allison's temple. My mother might see herself more clearly with an early afternoon drunk collapsed on the floor beside her shopping cart. Who you live with is important.

* * *

That night, in the parking lot at the mall, my father was beaten after he left the garden center. It was near midnight when he called me from the hospital. "I'm in a spot here," he said. "They're keeping me for observation, but I'll need a ride by sundown. The car's at the mall. You can walk there. It's only a mile from your school. Go for half a day and then drive it over here. I'll be fine by myself. There's nothing to see here."

My father was on the television news and in the morning paper, but I turned the television off and tried going back to bed. It didn't matter if I stayed home from school. It was just review now for tests, or else movies, as if watching *Saving Private Ryan* for three days was a history lesson, or *Good Will Hunting* was an English assignment instead of a way to kill time until test week.

I wanted to fall asleep, but I just lay there with my eyes shut. I knew my mother watched the news like she did every morning, drinking coffee and eating two cherry Danishes while she sat through what was called the second edition, the one-hour, 9:00 a.m. broadcast that included twenty minutes of features for women. After what I thought was more than an hour, I looked at the clock radio. Nine forty-six, it said, and I watched the numbers change until it read 10:15 without the phone ringing.

At 10:35, the phone rang, and I picked it up during the second ring. "How's Mr. Wheeler doing?" the female voice said. It could have been anyone but my mother. It could have been any teacher or neighbor or student. I hung up without answering and waited to hear whether it would ring again. I could have called my mother then, but I didn't. She was going to show up at the hospital or not. If I called, I wouldn't know what she would have done on her own. She had her chance to act, and I was doing my part to make it her choice.

Because I was starting from our house, I had to walk three miles to get to the mall, two of them along the shoulder of the four-lane highway, the traffic roaring by at fifty-five or more. I kept my eye on the trucks, closed my eyes against the grit they swirled up around me. I'd never seen anyone on foot along that road except men with ragged beards carrying a trash bag or two while they stuck out their thumbs as if somebody would give them a ride.

* * *

At the hospital, my father told me he had a concussion and two cracked ribs. There was a welt on the cheekbone so close to his eye I could imagine it torn from its socket. My father watched me as if he could figure out his condition by how I stood or moved my hands. It was the way you'd look at your boss, I thought, and I shoved my hands into my pockets like I was standing in the hall after class. My father pressed his lips together and reached for the cup of water that sat beside his bed. "They were boys," he finally said. "So I know it was Jessie Grant and three others."

"They wore ski masks, dad."

My father frowned. "Where did you hear that?" he asked.

"On the news."

"Of course," he said at once, but he looked thoughtful for a moment, as if he was trying to decide whether or not I'd heard that detail at school. "You can tell boys by their bodies, Jeff. None of them were filled out; even the heavy one looked young."

My father was as sure of his ID as he was of everything else, but the police, he said, claimed they needed more than his certainty. The assailants had all worn gloves. There wasn't much chance the police would find Jessie Grant's knuckles split. Those gloves were in a dumpster or the river. Jessie Grant, the police had said when they revisited him an hour before I'd arrived, was walking into school carrying three books like an ordinary student when they spotted him. The boy with him was heavy and empty handed, but the police had counted eight other boys his size while they talked to Jessie Grant.

I sat there all afternoon except for when I wandered off to the bathroom, taking a few minutes in the hospital's gift shop where books with the words *hope* and *recovery* were arranged on a stand that spun. Nearby were dozens of stuffed animals and hand puppets, all of them with the same cheerful smile on their faces. "For once, leaving is a good thing," was inscribed on a set of small plaques, and I tried to imagine what father-as-patient would welcome such a gift from his son. When my mother had left for good, I'd followed her to her car. I knew she had suitcases in the trunk, and there were liquor store boxes filling the back seat. The front seat was empty, though, and it seemed like an invitation rather than a sign she'd run out of things to take with her.

She got in the car and rolled the window down. "I can't come back now," she said. She reached out and laid her hand on mine and drew it to her lips. She held it there for a few seconds. "I know who I am," she said. "There's no mistaking that. I don't need your father to put a name to things."

I leaned down when she let go of my hand, but before I could speak, she rolled the window up. She rapped on the closed window and gave me a thumbs-up salute, something so out of character that I expected her to get back out of the car, hug me, and carry her suitcases inside like I'd passed some sort of test. And then she backed out and drove off without sounding the horn or waving.

I was gone less than ten minutes, so I was certain that no one visited. "By the time word gets out, I'll be out of here," my father said late in the afternoon.

I walked downstairs at five o'clock because the doctor had returned to run his checks on my father one last time. When I came back in half an hour, the doctor was gone, but he had a visitor, the woman who had been punched. I recognized her from school. Her name was Janet Longo.

I waited in the hall, walking past rooms where families were sitting around beds. The third time I looped around toward my father's room, Janet Longo was coming down the hall. "I know your father," she said, slowing down as she approached. "Now he won't be able to brag that I never showed appreciation."

She paused as if she expected me to argue, but I was looking at her stomach, noticing how she was going to fat under her loose fitting blouse. She was years younger than my father, maybe thirty-five, and I thought her shapelessness had something to do with being punched, that if she was trim in the middle no one would think of punching her.

"Well then," she added at last, and I nodded. My mother, at forty-five and a heavy drinker, had a better body than this woman, and it occurred to me that my father had misplaced his chivalry.

My father was on his feet when I walked into the room. "This should do it now," he said. "This particular game is over."

"OK," I said, and I looked away.

I heard my father breathing behind me, shallow, tight gasps that sounded like how you'd breathe if you were trapped underground. When I turned around, he was holding a book in his hand. "Janet Longo gave me this," he said. I could see the cover had a rainbow on it, but I couldn't make out the title to see if it said "hope" or "recovery" in it. "I was going to throw it just now, but my ribs wouldn't let me."

***

"I'm feeling a little peaked," my father said on the way home. "You'll have to mind the store for a day or two until I get my feet back under me."

"No problem," I said.

"It was a surprise to see Janet Longo walk in, I'll say that."

"We talked."

My father glanced at me and smiled. "Did you now?" He sat up a bit, grimacing. "She's taking her sick days and then quitting," he said. "Isn't that something? I told her I wished her well, but it near broke my heart to hear that straight from her mouth."

His voice kept going small at the end of his sentences. He didn't seem to be able to get enough air sitting down like he had to in the car seat, and he was quiet for a minute. I could tell he was trying to manage a full breath, one of those kinds you take for the doctor when he has a stethoscope to your chest.

"I had Jim Allison's son in class four years ago," he finally said. "He was something."

"I don't know him," I said.

His chest rose and fell a few times. "I would have had you next year," he said. "There's no getting around me when you're a senior."

"I know."

"Back when I had Jim Allison's boy, I wasn't thinking of you or your mother," my father said, and then he worked to sit himself up straighter, leaning back against the seat, I thought, to take the pressure off his ribs.

"There's no going back, is there?" he said.

"I guess not."

"I feel like I'm all square at school now, but it's likely that's finished."

His words were turning so soft I rolled the window up to hear better, and my father, as if he'd been waiting for the world to quiet down, said, "It makes you wonder if anything can be set right, doesn't it?"

"Seems like," I said, and right then I thought he was going to ask if my mother had called, but he didn't.

It was only 7:30 when we got to the house, but my father said he was going to bed. "These painkillers take the wind out of your sails," he said. Ten minutes later he was sound asleep.

I drove to the mall and walked to the household goods section of the store where my father worked. I was carrying his employee discount card, and after I'd chosen two gallons of paint, a roller, and a small brush, I showed it to the clerk. "My father asked me to get these things for him," I said.

"Should we check with him?" the clerk said.

"He's in the garden center," I said. I knew the truth would complicate things.

The clerk glanced past me as if he could see through appliances and electronics to where my father would be standing. "It's a Father's Day present," I went on. "I'm going to do the painting."

The clerk relaxed and smiled. "OK then," he said, and he lifted a package from the shelf behind him. "You'll need a drop cloth," he went on. "And let me give you some pointers so he'll be happy with your work."

When I arrived home, my father looked exactly the same in his bed. I moved all of the furniture into the center of the room like the clerk had suggested and covered it with the drop cloth. I stretched tape along the baseboards and unscrewed the light sockets exactly like the clerk had instructed me.

It was a good thing I'd listened to the instructions. I spattered paint on nearly every part of the drop cloth. I felt drops hit my face and saw them sprinkle my arms. I didn't stop to inspect myself. I kept going until the ceiling and the upper part of each wall were finished. I could reach everything else while standing on the floor.

I stood in the doorway to my father's room and listened to him breathe, and then I took the drop cloth outside and laid it on the porch before I arranged newspaper along the baseboards. That was enough protection now. I went into the bathroom and cleaned my face. I looked like a little boy with all that paint spattered on me, and I washed it off and went back to work. If my father woke and came out while I was working, he'd look up at the ceiling and down at the furniture and nod, and then he'd give me the once over and smile because he'd see that I'd been so careful I hardly looked like I'd been painting.

The walls were easy. I imagined my father sitting on the couch in the middle of the room watching me. I had the hang of the roller, how much paint to take on so it covered without dripping. Tomorrow morning, first thing, I'd move the furniture back, and the living room would be shipshape. If my father woke before I did, he'd see that I'd done the job right.

HOUSEHOLD HINTS

DURING THE WINTER OF THE heaviest snowfall ever in Central Pennsylvania, just after the roads were finally opened after five days of snow emergency, Gordon Benson opened his front door and was served a warrant for a long-delinquent parking violation.

Benson had spoken with the constable on the phone about this very same unpaid fine. Months ago. And he'd voluntarily driven to the magistrate's office to explain to the magistrate, with that constable present, what seemed to be the smallest of situations. Some employee of the dealership where his car was in for service had parked Benson's car facing the wrong way on a borough street. The ticket had blown away or been taken by pranksters walking past, and Benson had driven the car for months without knowing he owed fifteen dollars with penalties accumulating.

Benson had talked the dealership into writing a check for the fifteen dollars and carried it to the magistrate. He'd presented the check. Easy enough until he'd been told that those accumulated penalties now totaled sixty-five dollars, something he believed he couldn't be held responsible for, given that he'd never laid eyes on the parking ticket.

His wife already knew that much of the story. After he called from the county prison, Melissa drove on the snow-packed street, the plowed walls of it looming on both sides. "All of this for sixty-five dollars?" she said. "I saw exactly one car on my way over here, and it's eight miles. One. That should tell you something."

Benson didn't say there was more to tell. He was due at the bank at 8:15, and it was after midnight. The new chapter of his story could wait. "Thanks for coming," he said.

"Like I'm your buddy," she said. "Who else would come? Larry Abrams?"

She was right. Abrams was his buddy, his only one from work because Abrams was the only other man at the bank. Benson was a loan officer, after all, and prison, even for a few hours, was something to keep from the people who sat in front of him asking to acquire mortgages or loans for cars or college tuition money. Abrams was about to retire. He lived alone and, as far as Benson knew, didn't talk to anybody at the bank but him, and then only when the two of them walked three blocks down and across the street on Fridays at four o'clock to drink beer together.

"Jail," Melissa said. "You were in jail." And then she concentrated on the eight miles of icy highway.

***

Benson kept his arrest to himself throughout the spring. Larry Abrams was retiring before the end of the year, but Benson needed his job for the foreseeable future. He had two children in college—a freshman and a junior. His wife sold real estate, but she was on strict commission during a housing downturn, and lately she'd become a part-time mystery muncher, someone who was occasionally paid to order food from restaurants and fast food outlets as a sort of quality control. She filled out forms that asked her to rate the food and the service and the cleanliness of the business. In April, Benson did it for her once when she was asked to go back to Taco Bell for the third time. "I hate Mexican," she'd said. "You love it."

Benson purchased an assortment of items. The girl who waited on him was pleasant and cheerful. The restroom was clean. He took one bite of each item and tossed the rest into the trash can outside of the department store where he'd parked. He gave everything a high mark. People loved this crap, he thought. Just because it was awful didn't mean they weren't getting what they paid for.

Mystery munching was like detective work, ferreting out the guilty. So was banking, at least his side of it, privately examining assets and debts, looking for signs that applicants would fail to repay. The public side seemed to be women's work. Abrams had joked about it because every teller but him was a woman. In a way, they were buddies by default, and yet Abrams was effeminate, soft really, the kind of man Benson ordinarily avoided. But Abrams was a drinker with a man's appetite. He kept up with Benson. He drove three miles home every Friday at six o'clock without ever being stopped because, like Benson, he knew, after two hours of beer, how to control the impulse to speed or go so slowly that the police would notice his unnatural care.

And Abrams curbed Benson's compulsion to mock customers and employees. "A Weeble," Benson had said about Marlene Huff, the fat teller; "Olive Oyl," he'd said about the anorexic woman who'd carried fifty rolls of pennies to where, nearly a year ago, Abrams was standing one Friday, and Abrams, both times, had nodded and said, "That's true," with so little inflection that Benson had felt shame.

The only thing Abrams ridiculed was authority—politicians, the military, the police. "Filth," he said without elaborating. He'd had a run-in sometime, Benson thought, and some day he'd volunteer his reasons, just like he'd volunteered, shortly after they'd started drinking together, that he'd worked at the bank for thirteen years, starting there when his office supplies and typewriter repair business had failed. "Typewriter repair," Abrams had said. "It sounded like a good idea in 1969, and it was for about twenty years." Benson could imagine the details. He'd started a year and a half ago, promoted and transferred from across the state just in time to pay for college bills.

* * *

Abrams invited Benson and Melissa to his house in the early summer. He lived along the river among a cluster of small houses that, except for his, were used mostly as summer homes. Melissa brought flowers, a cluster of iris she'd taken from their yard. "They're beautiful," Abrams said. "I'll put them in water. Just give me a second."

When Abrams returned, he dropped a charcoal briquette into the half-filled vase before he laid the stems into the water. "What's that all about?" Melissa said.

"They last longer with charcoal in the water. You'd be surprised how well it works." Abrams handed Benson a beer and poured a glass of wine for Melissa. "The way Gordon talks about you, I figured a dry white," he said, and Melissa smiled and glanced at Benson with a look that reminded him he'd never once bought her a bottle of wine, leaving her drinking choices up to her.

Holding his own beer, Abrams walked them down to where the river lapped against the bank a few feet below where the backyard ended. "It's beautiful," Melissa said. "I can see why you live here."

"Partially because it was so cheap," Abrams said. "I bought it a month after the ninety-six flood. The owner just wanted out."

"Floods," Melissa said. "I guess that's part of living here. Was it bad?"

"There was an ice jam and a bout of late January rain. A bad combination. It came up fast and ruined everything the fellow owned." Abrams shook his can and frowned. "The tour guide needs a refill. You guys can stay here and enjoy while I go check on dinner."

"We'll come in when we're empty," Benson said, trying for a laugh, but Abrams was already halfway across the small lawn.

A half hour later Abrams served a small ham and baked beans. The meat was pressed into a snub-nosed triangle, and Benson imagined the can it had come in stuffed in the garbage, its shape identical. While Abrams sliced it at the table with a steak knife, Benson noticed that Abrams had switched to wine.

The meal was awkward, the meat rubbery, the beans familiar. No one wanted seconds. But after Abrams cleared the table, he carried in a red raspberry pie. "You baked this?" Melissa said at once.

"From scratch," he said. "Meat for one is hard," he said, "but dessert, as long as you make something that keeps, is easy."

The crust, Benson had to admit, was perfect. Light and crisp. "After a few tries, you learn to make crust, how to use a rolling pin. And raspberries are perfect because they're tart; they make for a better flavor, especially if you add barely any sugar."

"Such a homemaker," Benson said, and Melissa gave him a look that said, "Shut up."

"You learn," Abrams said good-naturedly. "It's like knowing about anything around the house."

"Like what?" Melissa said. She was looking at the flowers on the counter as if she could detect how perky they were.

"Fluorescent lights, maybe," Abrams said, nodding toward the pair of them that framed the stove. "When one end of a tube goes dark, reverse it. You'll be pleased about how it's restored."

"Well, I'm not much for fluorescent lights, but this pie is fantastic," Melissa said, "and yes, I'll have another glass of wine now that you're pouring one for yourself."

Abrams smiled. "I should have let the pie set for a few more minutes," he said. "It's run just a bit." He really is effeminate, Benson thought. Like a wife. Like somebody Melissa would call on the phone to gossip with in the afternoon.

"You know your details," Melissa said. "Gordon told me how you could remember every last thing about the robber you had last fall."

"That wasn't hard. He hissed his *s*'s; he had a short stride, like his shoes were too tight. Not a limp, just truncated."

"See there," Melissa said, turning toward Benson as if he was going to be called as a witness.

Abrams drank off half of his wine. He's drunk, Benson

guessed. He was drinking before we arrived. Nervous, maybe, about meeting Melissa or having people inside his house. "The guy was left-handed, and there was a ring scar, his skin pale there on one finger the way a man takes off his wedding ring when he goes out trolling for women. And his fingernails were yellow and thick, like horns."

"It didn't matter in the end," Benson heard himself saying. "The guy drove off in a green Ford with a gray door and a set of NASCAR number eight decals along one side. A Dale Earnhardt fan. Like worshipping Elvis or something."

"But it's way more interesting to identify somebody by subtle things," Melissa said.

"It's because I hate to be told to do anything," Abrams said. "As soon as he showed the gun I was memorizing."

* * *

Melissa called Abrams two weeks later and invited him for dinner. "We'll have spaghetti," she said. "I'll use sauce straight from the jar. We don't want to embarrass him."

"But you'll make a pie?"

Melissa glanced at the phone as if the connection was still open. "You can't be jealous, can you? Your friend is gay."

"How do you know that? Because he makes pies?"

"You're so unobservant. Just pay attention. Learn something. Did you even notice the bright spots on his living room wall?"

Benson looked around the kitchen. It seemed unfamiliar, as if Melissa had rearranged things before he crawled out of bed. He shrugged. "No."

"You never notice these things. They were all rectangles—where photographs used to hang."

"Or paintings?"

"These were all photo size, Gordon. You know, eight by ten. There were six of them altogether. I counted. Why would he take them down?"

"Maybe they've been down for a while."

"The contrast was sharp. I felt like they were stacked up in his bedroom or something waiting for us to leave. How do you miss these things?"

* * *

After they'd finished their spaghetti, Melissa served a lemon cake. "I didn't want to chance ruining a pie crust," she said. "A cake is so much easier."

"It's excellent," Abrams said. "I'll help you clear."

Benson hurried to gather his own plate and fork, following them to the kitchen. "Oh my God," he heard Melissa say.

What looked to be a hundred ants were crawling where Melissa had left, apparently, a few splatters of sweetness near the sink. She tried to wipe them away with a dishcloth, but Benson could see there were dozens more.

"Put a little sugar on that damp cloth," Abrams said. "Get them all into one place before you try to deal with them."

Melissa soaked the cloth and spooned sugar onto it without questioning Abrams. Abrams pushed his used cake plate in front of her, and she laid the cloth upon it. "Good," Abrams said. "Now let's give them some time to congregate." Abrams nodded toward the sink. "It's all about getting them to swarm to one spot. They'll be there soon enough. Then it's just a matter of plunging the cloth and plate into boiling water."

"Or you could just spray the shit out of them with Raid?"

"You don't want that poison in your kitchen."

Melissa poured water into the pot she'd used to cook the spaghetti. "Medium hot," Abrams said. "Give the little shits some time."

They carried drinks onto the deck. Abrams said, "Something most people don't know, but ants hate cucumbers. It's as if they're allergic. Bits of the skin will clear places they swarm. And they hate chalk, too." Abrams was rolling. Expansive. He sounded like a chef on the food channel, someone with the authority of being filmed behind him.

"Really?" Melissa said. "What else do you know about ants?"

"That's all."

Twenty minutes later, when there were still stragglers milling around on the counter after a hundred or more ants had been boiled, Benson was happy. It took three sugar traps to wipe out the ants. "An hour," he told Melissa after Abrams left. "Who has an hour to fool with ants?"

"Don't you like that it was an organic solution?"

"I hope that means you're drunk," Benson said, and Melissa laughed, a girlish giggle that made him cringe.

"He's your friend, Gordon," she said. "I wanted him to feel at home."

* * *

The next Friday afternoon, Abrams said, "Sorry your wife had the ant invasion." He touched glasses with Benson. "I know you can't stand hearing me play homebody. It's not special. If you lived by yourself, you'd know these things, too. It's the middle of August and hot as hell. Come out to the river with me, just you, and we'll go out in my canoe. No women stuff. None whatsoever."

Benson put it off for two weeks. Abrams looked frail to him, like maybe he had a reason to retire besides closing in on sixty-five. And he didn't want to be in a canoe. "You'll be safer than in your car," Abrams said, holding the canoe steady as it rocked slightly in the shallow water at the river's edge.

"Like flying, right?"

"Safer than that."

"I don't swim."

"There's a life jacket."

"That's OK—you enjoy. I'll watch you from here and drink up all your beer."

"I guess that's what we'll do then," Abrams said. "Watch and drink. Christ, in three months that's all I'll be doing."

Suddenly, Benson thought Abrams wouldn't be asking him back, that he'd ruined some sort of protocol. "I'll miss the four-oh-fives," he said, trying to soften the moment.

"I'll drive in on Fridays," Abrams said, brightening. He snapped open two more beers as if the canoe incident was closed now.

"The bank will hire a man to replace you," Benson said. "They have to."

"If there's a man out there who's willing," Abrams said. "Someone like you gets to decide what happens to the bank's money, part of it, anyway. All I do is enter numbers."

"But they have to be correct."

"It's work for a twelve-year-old."

"A responsible one. They're rare."

"Not that rare. The problem wouldn't be the numbers; it would be people having a hard time handing over their money to a kid. It would make it seem like play money, like they were playing a board game."

"We can't let them know, then, can we?"

On his way home, Benson appreciated Abrams' drunk driving skills. There were nine stop signs, two yields, and a host of intersections to navigate. "Did he have the photos back up?" Melissa asked when he walked in.

"I didn't go inside."

"You drank beer with him for nearly three hours. You had to go inside."

"OK, but I never thought about it. The walls must have looked the same or I'd have noticed. Don't you think?"

"I think you're lucky to be in one piece, that it's a good thing you don't have two friends like Larry Abrams."

* * *

The next Friday, at five thirty, Abrams held up his newly filled mug and said, "It's an anniversary. A year now."

Benson kept his mug on the bar. "I've worked here longer than that."

"Not that. The important one, the first Friday beer call." He lifted his mug and they touched glasses in salute.

"What do you give for a first anniversary?" Benson said. He was pleasantly buzzed and willing to let Abrams educate him about some other womanly trivia.

"Paper," Abrams said.

"I'm sure that never happened at my house. We probably went out for dinner at some place with cloth napkins."

Abrams looked serious. "It should have. You only get the one chance."

"I did silver last year. Jewelry. I know all about that one." Benson looked around. The bar was getting crowded like it always did after five. "And the dinner, too," he added. "I didn't subtract anything just because I was splurging."

"Good," Abrams said. "It's good to live with someone."

Benson waited, happy to have the beer to concentrate on while Abrams reached under his stool and came up with an envelope that he handed to Benson. "Paper. See? As a friend. Nothing else."

Benson marveled. The card had been lying on the floor for nearly two hours. He slid it out of the envelope and looked at the cartoonish picture of a couple in a canoe. Inside, the card had the woman saying, "What anniversary has a gift of water?"

"There's a story that goes with this," Abrams said. "Nearly three years ago now, before you moved here, I was beaten by a cop."

"By the river?" Benson said.

"No, but it could just have well have been." Abrams glanced at the card as if what he planned on saying was written on the back. He took a breath and began again. "It was at the county park twenty miles from here. Maybe you've been there. It's a beautiful place, but it's also where I drive sometimes, you know, a place where men cruise, and I'm not likely to run into somebody I know."

Benson closed the card and laid it on the bar. He picked it up again, but held it face down as Abrams went on. "This guy I hooked up with thought that's exactly what had happened, that I recognized him. He was a cop, so he said he was working undercover and arrested me for indecent exposure, but first he hit me a few times. With his fist. So he could say he had to fend me off. It was mutual, I can tell you that. His thing about being undercover was bullshit. That cop is a cocksucker, too. He had a ring on—I always look. And you know what, he was right. The guy comes into our bank once or twice a month. He always goes to Marlene's or one of the other women's windows. He cuffed me and did another guy to make it look good. He hauled two of us in. They put our names in the paper but not his. I was sixty-one back then, but you'd be surprised how many men that age are cruising. That cop had to be at least fifty."

"I thought that sort of thing was over," Benson said. "I thought gay men could be more open and all."

"This is rural Pennsylvania, Gordon." Abrams lifted the card from Benson's hand, but didn't open it. "That wasn't the first time." He handed the card back to Benson, nodding toward the tables where a few diners had settled in. "And not the second."

Benson almost opened the card again. He had to say something. "You know what," he blurted, "Sunday will be my one-week anniversary for ironing."

Abrams didn't say anything, but he seemed to relax a bit, and Benson went on. "I think it's your influence or something. Melissa all of a sudden told me it was time for me to start doing my own ironing."

"You could make a case she should have said that a long time ago."

"That's not the influence part. It was the way she went on about it. You know, the instructions, how if I was doing a shirt, I should start with the collar first, both sides, before pressing the back and front of sleeves, then the rest until it's wrinkle-free. It was like she was moving out or something, the way she was teaching me. For pants, she said it was the pockets first, then the waistband, butt, and crotch. The legs go last, inseams aligned. 'Hang everything up right away,' she said. 'Always give them space because cooling sets the press.'"

"Now you know," Abrams said. "It's nothing any man can't do."

* * *

Near the end of September the weather channel spent six days tracking a late hurricane that was coming up the east coast. The wind was dissipating, but there was going to be two days, at least, of steady, heavy rain, which started, exactly on schedule, Thursday afternoon. "They want me to evacuate," Abrams said as they settled in Friday at 4:05, the bar nearly deserted.

"So?"

"The cops want their jobs easier. If nobody's there, they can put up a barricade and drink coffee. But I'm being cautious. You'll see. I'm leaving after three slow beers. One hour and I'm gone. There's plenty of time for me to decide."

"You should leave if they tell you to," Benson said.

"I know my own house and its limits."

"Good."

"The police. Fuck."

Abrams kept his promise. It was quarter to five before they ordered a third round, Benson holding back to be good company. The bartender placed the mugs on paper napkins. "You should know they're talking in the back about closing early. People have property to take care of, and there sure as hell isn't much business to lose, you two and those two fellows that have been down there since three."

"I'm out of here on the hour," Abrams said. He waved his mug toward the window. "No worries driving, that's for sure. Nobody's out giving tickets tonight."

Benson finished his beer quickly, checking the clock to see that it was 4:55. "I only have a few minutes," he said, "but I've been saving this story for a while, and it feels like right now, in the next five minutes, is when I ought to tell it. Only Melissa knows. I was in jail once right here in town." Abrams nodded like it wasn't unusual, and Benson rolled the parking ticket story out, racing through the events until he got to when the magistrate, the night the warrant was served, declared, "Sixty-five dollars or five days in prison."

Benson glanced at the clock. 4:58. He had enough time to finish. "I said I'd take the five days. Just like that because I was so pissed. It was only when I was being processed that I knew I needed to pay up. I spent an hour and a half with prisoners who were in for not paying child support, for driving drunk repeatedly, for welfare fraud. They were all being housed in a sort of ward, you know, cots laid out in a row. The only other thing there was a Ping-Pong table. That's what I did. I played Ping-Pong. I won five games in a row before Melissa showed up because no one else knew to put top spin on the ball."

"Scofflaw," Abrams said. "That's what they call that."

"Fantastic, right? A parking ticket."

"I believe every word." Abrams swallowed his beer and smiled. "I liked the part where you refused to pay. Couldn't you have called in sick for three days and used the weekend for the other two?" He raised the mug again, but noticed it was empty. "It's your turn to pay the tab, and you're getting off light."

"I'll pay next time, too."

"I'll hold you to that."

Abrams disappeared into the rain, but Benson sat by himself, ordering one more. One of the other two men leaned toward him from halfway down the bar. "Lover's quarrel?" he said.

"What?"

"Whatever," the man said and turned away. Benson threw down enough to cover a 20 percent tip and left, relieved not to have to pass along the bar.

It was still pouring. "Expected to stop by early evening," the radio said, "but the river won't crest until tomorrow afternoon."

"Home early?" Melissa said. "It's nice to see you have some good judgment on a Friday afternoon."

"I guess," Benson said. He looked at Melissa. "Here's a question for you. If you drink with a friend who's gay, do strangers assume you're gay?"

"If they're morons."

"So who cares, right?"

"Gordon," Melissa said, "there are a lot of morons out there. Why, you get propositioned?"

"Name-called."

"Straight out? Just like that?"

"By implication."

"In this part of the country," she said, "count yourself lucky."

The phone rang, and Benson, standing right beside it, picked up. "Hey," he heard Abrams say, "they're all in a dither down this way. The cops are telling us to leave."

"So leave, right?" Benson said.

"I'm going to read for a while and then reevaluate."

Benson saw that Melissa was listening. "Come and stay with us if you want," he said, and she nodded.

"Believe it or not, I have an attic," Abrams said. "Not much of one, but there's some headroom in the middle and I can get by up there. But I'd feel really shut up, nothing but water underneath me for Christ knows how long."

"Think about my offer."

"I surely will, but not right this second when the cops are acting like they know more than everybody."

Benson hung up and turned on the television news. The flood report was over. At 5:25, a woman was doing a puff piece in a series called "Household Hints."

Benson watched as the camera panned from the ceiling down to the floor of the room in which she was standing. "Tonight's episode is 'How to Clean a Room,'" she said. "This one is simple: From top to bottom, beginning with ceiling fans, tops of cupboards, and the cobwebs in high corners. The filth will fall at your feet where you'll finish, ending with carpets."

Benson turned it off and stared outside, where the weather, as far as he could tell, hadn't changed all day.

***

In the morning, the rain became a sporadic drizzle, and Benson stood at a back window, astonished at how his backyard was a small lake up to within a few feet of the house. "It's a lot of rain to do that," Melissa said.

Benson opened the window and exhaled. "It's like Florida or something," he said.

"Exactly," Melissa said. "Think about where all this came from." The doorbell chimed, and she took three steps before she stopped and said, "It's a policeman, Gordon. You answer."

She gripped his arm. "Which of them?" she whispered. "Which one?"

Benson picked their son, the junior, but he didn't say anything. He pulled her hand away and walked to the door. "Do you know a Lawrence Abrams," the policeman said as soon as the door was open, and Benson, now that he knew it wasn't one of his children who had been injured or killed, looked closely at the policeman because he appeared to be in his fifties, graying.

"Yes." This could be the guy who'd arrested Abrams, Benson thought, but why come here?

"Did he by any chance spend the night here?"

"No."

"He's missing," the policeman said, and Benson sagged, looking back at Melissa, who mouthed, "What?" and began to move closer.

"It's not the kids," he said at once, putting one arm around her and turning back to face the policeman, who started in again.

"His car was discovered unattended this morning not far from his home. We're in the process of contacting friends and coworkers, those with whom he may have found shelter."

"Larry?" Melissa said. "Did he drown?"

"We don't know that for certain," the policeman said. "Thank you for your trouble."

* * *

Benson and Melissa watched the noon news and the six o'clock news, but there was no mention of flood victims. "Maybe he's safe then," Melissa said at 6:30, but at ten o'clock, the second story was about the body of Lawrence Abrams being found jammed under a car near his home along the river. "Mr. Abrams's body was discovered by a neighbor who had been allowed back onto his property early this evening to retrieve personal items from his evacuated house," the newscaster said. "It appears as if his car stalled in the rushing flood water, and when he stepped out, the current swept him off his feet and under the car."

There was an interview with a rescue worker, who commented, near the end. "I hate to say this, but if Mr. Abrams had not left at all, he could have ridden this out in his home. Flood damage, sure, but it's not like he'd have been more than up to his knees inside his house."

They walked out onto the deck. The lights from the house reflected off the shrinking pools of water in the yard in a way that seemed picturesque. "He waited just a bit too long," Melissa said.

"It's not about the timing," Benson said. "I think he was sick. I think that's why he decided to leave instead of riding it out, and then I think he didn't have the strength to keep himself on his feet."

"So you think you noticed something?"

"There has to be more to it. The car could stall and sit there, but all he had to do was go back into the house and climb the stairs."

Melissa took his hand and squeezed it. "That water was running really fast."

"What do you know about the speed of water?"

"As much as you do, Gordon."

$$* * *$$

On Sunday morning Benson drove to the river, pausing at the head of Abrams's street because a policeman was flagging him down. "You have business here?" the policeman said, leaning close as Benson rolled down his window.

"Yes," Benson began, but the policeman rapped the top of the car twice with his fist. "You're the parking ticket desperado," he said. "You were the talk of the station for a few days. You have a place down this way?"

"A friend does. I'm here to help."

The policeman nodded, and Benson looked at him again, but he didn't look at all familiar. If he'd been fighting the ticket, Abrams would have known this cop immediately, Benson thought, but right now he wasn't sure if this was the cop who'd processed him or just another guy who'd been in the station. "It's no fun mucking a place out," the policeman said.

Benson looked down the street, then back at the policeman. "People aren't who you think they are," he said, and inched forward before the cop could give him the go-ahead, his cliché dissipating like a bad smell the cop didn't even acknowledge, not out of politeness, but out of indifference. He accelerated slightly, his eyes at the side view mirror to see if the cop would pursue him, but already the policeman had turned away.

Benson drove to where Abrams's short driveway ended. He pulled in and backed out and stopped where he imagined the car must have stalled as Abrams shifted from reverse to drive in water that must have been channeled swift and deep by the slight downslope of asphalt.

He pushed his car door open and stepped out into where the flood had caught Abrams by the ankles and swept him to lodge under a car parked nearly a hundred feet away. Benson thought of that small canned ham that Abrams had carried out on a plate, how it had sat there on the coffee table with a knife and fork beside it as if it was a twenty-five pound Thanksgiving turkey to be carved.

And then Benson left his car idling with the door open and walked to the end of the street where a car was parked in a bare spot at the end of the pavement. He knelt as if he were reaching for something that had rolled underneath. The clearance didn't seem high enough to catch a body. Abrams had to have hit his head. He had to be unconscious as he was swept here.

Benson heard a sound and looked at the nearest house. What would he say if the owner came out and asked him what he was doing? Maybe he'd tell that owner to fuck off, start a series of exchanges that would send him to jail again.

He leaned farther down, disgusted at himself. He wouldn't do anything but apologize. He wouldn't do anything but retreat from the selfishness of being there. If that cop drove down the street he'd see Benson on his knees like a man surrendering.

He was ashamed of his brush with petty crime. He might as

well have told Abrams about stealing change from his mother's purse when he was a boy, always making sure not to take more than twenty cents in pennies, nickels, and dimes, waiting between thefts so it took two weeks to steal a dollar.

He pushed himself upright and stood at the edge of Abrams's yard, his car still idling a few feet away. With Abrams dead, who would clean the house? Prepare it for viewing? "From top to bottom," Benson remembered.

He drifted up the walk to Abrams's front door. There was a chance he could see if the photographs were hanging, and Benson imagined that they would be photos of Abrams and the man he'd loved, that they'd be there now because Abrams had told him the story of being beaten by the homosexual cop. He tried the door, but of course it was locked, and though the drapes were parted, Benson didn't press his face close to the living room window to see inside. It wasn't a lack of nerve, he told himself. It was because he was afraid the frames would be around magazine pictures Abrams had cut out, landscapes and such, so cheap-looking Abrams had taken them down before Benson and Melissa had arrived, embarrassed because anyone who claimed to be able to take care of a house should never have such pictures on his living room wall.

SAINTS

SALVATORE

ON THE SECOND FLOOR OF Our Lady of Angels School, in Room 211, Salvatore Crisci passes a note to Angela Nicolazzo, who holds it in her fist for a minute, making sure Sister Bernice hasn't noticed. Like she always does, Angela looks straight ahead as she passes it on to Mary Tomzak, who slides it under her skirt, just beneath her right thigh. For thirty seconds, while it lies hidden, Sal concentrates on not staring directly at that spot, but a moment later, when Mary slips it out between two fingers, unfolds it inside her notebook, and reads, he breathes more slowly and smiles.

This is the sixth day of their note passing, and by now, without ever looking his way, Mary is able to write an answer as if she's copying an assignment off the blackboard. It's been four minutes since he finished the note at 1:57 just as everyone put their history books away to get ready for silent reading, a story about St. Bernadette and the miracles at Lourdes. They are expected to write a report on it for next Monday.

Sal has stuffed the note he wrote first into his history book so he can throw it away after school. "I think I'm becoming devoted to you," it says, but it sounded like the Everly Brothers song from last summer, and they look too much like hicks to be cool. Stuck, he'd thought of a song his father loved. "I hope you keep that breathless smile forever," he wrote. "Never ever change. I love the way you look today." Unless her father owned the same record, Mary would never know a song that wasn't on the radio. Sal imagines her answer and how the letters will look below his message. Mary's handwriting is as perfect as Sister Bernice's.

ANTHONY

In the basement of Our Lady of Angels, just after two o'clock, Anthony Vicaro finishes his cigarette and drops the butt into the cardboard trash barrel at the foot of the stairs. It's an hour until he can smoke again, and already he's looking forward to it, another day of fifth grade over with, Christmas creeping closer. He slips a mint into his mouth as he climbs two flights of stairs back to Room 206. Monday, at least, is almost over, he thinks, imagining his cigarette starting a fire in all that trash, the janitor swearing as he throws water on it.

Give the guy something to do, Anthony thinks. Maybe scare the shit out of him. Before he opens the door that Sister Veronica unlocks for him, Anthony chews what is left of the mint so she won't notice he has something in his mouth. Maybe she's never had a fifth grader who smokes, he thinks. When she gives her monthly lecture about the filthy habit of smoking, she always talks about the eighth grade boys as if all of them were weed fiends. It's December 1—let her believe what she wants for the rest of the year so he can keep getting bathroom passes.

Thanksgiving has just slipped by—the Macy's parade from
New York on television, Chicago with its own parade that Sal
watched with his friends, pretending he thought it was only for
kids under twelve. Already everybody has begun to talk Christmas, and Sister Bernice has had to warn the class twice to settle
down since lunch. A third time means she will single someone
out to make an example of, rapping his wrists or the back of his
neck with a ruler. It's always a boy she strikes, though there are
girls who get scolded and made to stand in one place for half
an hour. There are seven rows with seven desks to a row, and
every one of those seats is filled. Despite Sister Bernice's com-
plaints, Sal knows they listen, at least when she's talking, like
children at Mass, and they are able to read by themselves from
two o'clock until two forty-five, when Sister Bernice will explain
their homework, answer questions, and dismiss them.

"Hush," Sister Bernice says. "Hush your mouth, Salvatore."
He hasn't said a word, and the boy behind him, Vincent Ruzomberka, the fattest boy in the class, begins to poke Sal in the
back with his pencil as soon as Sister Bernice turns to the blackboard where she's writing their assignments for tomorrow.

"Got a hard on?" Ruzomberka whispers, repeating what he's
said a few seconds ago as if Sal is supposed to answer.

Piggy, Sal thinks, but he doesn't risk the word aloud. Sister
Bernice will be keeping an eye on him until three o'clock. He
wants to read one more note from Mary and send her a reply
because today is when he has vowed to talk to her face to face.

In three hours Sal will have dinner to cook at home. His
mother has been sick for two weeks, unexplainable so far. His

father gave her the money to go to the doctor after the first three days, but she insists she is waiting to see how things shape up. "It's better some days," she told Sal last night. "We'll see what we will see." She made the turkey for Thanksgiving and baked two pumpkin pies. She picked at her food but drank a glass of wine and ate all the pumpkin out of her slice of pie. She's been in bed since then, though, and Salvatore's been using up everything in the refrigerator. Spaghetti with his mother's homemade sauce and chuck roast cooked with carrots and potatoes and onions. Tonight he is using up the pork chops and the eggplant. He wonders if Mary would be surprised that he cooks real food, something besides hot dogs and canned soup.

Sal decides "Yes" before he asks himself if she would think that is a good thing for a boy to be doing. His father has never cooked. So far Sal hasn't bought anything at the store except bread and milk. "There's nothing to be gained from panic," his mother has said each night she hasn't finished more than a few bites of anything Sal has cooked. Sal knows those are his father's words, ones he carried home with him from the war. By Wednesday there won't be anything left to cook, and Sal thinks this will be when his mother either gets out of bed or goes to the doctor.

MARY

Mary sits two rows away, so Angela Nicolazzo always helps to pass the notes between them. Mary knows that Angela is careful and doesn't read them like a boy would. Two hours ago at lunch Mary told Angela she thinks about Sal kissing her. "But first he has to talk," she said. "Why are the best boys always so shy?"

"The wait will be worth it," Angela said. Mary believes her because Angela has a boyfriend in tenth grade at the Catholic high school, and Mary has listened to her stories about making out. Mary has danced with two boys and held hands with one, and no matter what she tells Angela, she's glad that Sal acts like a boy with as little experience as she has.

SALVATORE

As Mary sits up to see where Sister Bernice is, Sal looks at the profile of her breasts, thinking, at once, that Vincent Ruzomberka is doing the exact same thing. Sal looks back at his book about how the Virgin Mother appeared eighteen times to Bernadette and tries to remember Mary without breasts. It's only been since last June, when school ended, but he barely remembers her from seventh grade. In the school picture from the year before she looks like someone he's never seen.

Now he carries her photograph in his shirt pocket. It's buttoned shut like all of the pockets on the white shirts he wears to school, which makes him check every shirt before he drops it into the laundry basket, afraid he's forgotten to remove the picture before it goes into the wash. The last time he saw his shirts hanging on the clothesline, wrung out but still dripping, he imagined Mary's picture still inside one of the pockets and patted the shirt he was wearing. It's been one week since then, and by Friday Sal will be out of white shirts even though he's worn each of them two days instead of one since then. He's never run clothes through the wringer. The weather is turning so cold he thinks his shirts, if he can manage to wash them right, will freeze on the line.

The note Sal will send if there is time before three o'clock will ask Mary for a second picture, one to put in a frame he bought over the weekend. When he talks out loud to her today, he will repeat his request for a second picture, something easy to say to get things started. He thinks of her writing "To Sal, Love, Mary" on the back. The one he already has from her is blank.

Two weeks ago, on the day their pictures came back from the photographer's studio, was when Mary had asked Sal for his picture and he had written her his first note. Sal's father allowed him to get only one dozen wallet size and one five by seven for the mantle. Eight of the dozen went to grandparents and uncles and aunts. He'd given three to his best friends when they went to the parade and the other one to Mary.

* * *

Even before she got sick, Sal's mother claimed she was an amateur martyr. "If things get bad enough," she would say, "I could be a saint." She laughed each time she brought it up, which was never when his father was nearby.

"What do you think about Saint Monica?" she said a month ago. "You know her—the patron saint of wives?"

Sal remembered how Saint Monica was the mother of Saint Augustine, a miracle in itself. "She must have been wonderful," he told his mother, "to raise a saint," and she hugged him.

"You're so smart," she said. "Thank God you're a boy. You'll have a chance to use that brain of yours."

That afternoon she told Sal how she'd won the commercial course award when she graduated from high school. "Ten silver dollars," she said. "In 1938 that was a fortune. Here I am twenty years out of high school, yet I still have each and every one of them. And I can still type and do shorthand, and don't you dare sign up for one of those classes at the high school next year."

She typed a page from the *Reader's Digest* as fast as Sal read it out loud, telling him first to go ahead and not worry about her "as long as you don't go to town on me." There was one overstrike on the page, her going back and putting in a *b* over a *v*. Sal didn't remember when she had doubled back, but she was upset about the error. "It's what I get for showing off," she said.

Yesterday, instead of citing Saint Monica, his mother brought up Saint Rita. "She's a good one, all right," she said, and Sal listened while she told him the story of how a thorn from the crucifix had lodged in Saint Rita's forehead and the wound had never healed, yet she had been happy to suffer like Jesus. "You know that story, don't you?" his mother said.

"Yes," Sal said. It sounded made-up to him, but Sal didn't tell her that even though he wanted her to stop talking before she got around to reminding him St. Rita was the patron of impossible causes.

* * *

Sal knows the stories of dozens of saints, but he is the only boy in his class who doesn't seem to recognize the models of the new cars by their fins and grille and chrome. Once he gets started, it will be easier to talk to Mary than to other boys. She won't expect him to know about cars or the Chicago Bears. She'll like music—the Chantels, Jerry Butler, maybe even "Oh Carol" or something else by Chuck Berry. He's started to watch shows like *Father Knows Best* and *Ozzie and Harriet*, sure she loves them.

While Mary and Angela were talking about him at lunch, Sal was half listening to the rest of his table about Chryslers and Pontiacs. John Guardino's father bought a new Chrysler every October when next year's model came out, and Guardino, muscular and a talker, was describing how cool this year's fins were while Sal stared at the table where Angela and Mary sat. "You bored, Crisci?" Guardino said across the lunch table. "Oh, that's right, your father doesn't own a car, so what do you care?"

Sal shrugged and finished his milk. Guardino looked across the room where Mary and Angela were sitting. "It's almost Christmas and Sal is feeling Mary," he said, and the other boys, including his friends, laughed.

"In his dreams," one of his friends said, and everybody laughed again.

"Fuck you," Sal said, the words so surprising inside the school they all looked around to see if anybody had heard. When no one swooped toward them, Guardino said, "Wouldn't you like to write that a hundred times on the board?" and even Sal laughed, happy to have said it and been lucky enough not to get caught.

The last boys Sister Bernice had caught passing a note filled the blackboard with "Duane Eddy is the coolest" and "Link Wray is the best." Beginning at 3:05, when everyone but Sister

Bernice was gone, they each had to write small enough to squeeze their sentences on one hundred times. In the morning the words were still there so the rest of the class knew they'd finished. After every tenth sentence there was a short blue line that the class knew was Sister Bernice counting to one hundred. While she checked homework, the two boys washed the blackboards, erasing their support for their favorite guitar players. Sal, if he was asked to vote to settle the argument, would choose Link Wray because his guitar sounds like it comes from the city, from some part of a neighborhood where his parents didn't allow him to go.

* * *

Angela is the only girl every boy, even John Guardino, is afraid to talk to. She is the only girl Sal has ever heard say the word "shit," and he knows that her passing notes for him means something very good. She is the only girl in the room who doesn't look embarrassed when she catches a boy staring at her. She is the girl Sal thinks of when he reaches for himself before sleep. When he passes or receives a note, he tries to avoid touching her fingers.

Once he talks to Mary, he thinks he will be able to talk to Angela. Let Guardino say something then. He won't have to know the model of some car Guardino points at while it's still three blocks away because it will be like he's already in high school, like he knows something way more important than the difference between a Chevy Bel Air and a Mercury Monterey.

MARY

After Mary slips the note back to Angela, she looks straight ahead at Sister Bernice, who immediately begins to walk up the aisle toward them. Mary holds her breath, and Angela keeps her hand closed over the note, but Sister passes by them to the door. Mary watches Sal reach out for the note from Angela and smells smoke. Sister Bernice stands by the double door as if she's listening. She opens the inside door and quickly closes it, but Mary sees there is smoke between the doors. She knows the outer one is always locked and the key is kept in Sister Bernice's desk in the front of the room. Two girls near the door cough, and Sister tells everybody to pay attention and stay in their seats.

ANTHONY

When he smells smoke, Anthony Vicaro looks at Sister Veronica before he can keep himself from doing something so stupid that will give him away. He shifts his eyes to the double door and sees that half the room is looking that way. He is the only one in his fifth-grade class she has ever caught with cigarettes, and he was out of the room twenty-five minutes ago. She is probably thinking of him already, how careless he might be, how she's warned him about "that filthy habit." They can't prove anything, he thinks, not even if the whole school burns to the ground. If the janitor needs help putting it out, his class will be useless. Sister Veronica isn't tall enough to lift a fire extinguisher off the wall. Nobody in their class is. Anthony knows everything like that is up high to keep kids from playing with it. Even the windowsills are up high so nobody can lean out and fall.

After a minute he is pretty sure there is enough smoke to bring the firemen. That will be the most exciting thing ever, Anthony thinks. It will be all everybody will talk about for days, and maybe, if they're lucky, school will be closed for the rest of the week.

SALVATORE

A hundred times, at least, Sal has heard his father say he considers himself a failure except for one thing, but his father has never told Sal what that one thing is any of those times he's said this while holding a glass of beer in his hands in the living room. Half of the time the television is on with no volume, the actors moving their mouths and their hands like something important is happening that Sal will never know about.

Even when Sal can barely hear a sound, his father asks him to turn off the volume. "Turn that down for me, would you?" he says, holding up his bottle of Blue Ribbon. "And get me another of these?"

Sal wishes he could say, "No," but he'd rather listen to his father say he is a failure than have his father tell him he is an ungrateful son of a bitch.

Last night, his father asked him to turn down Ed Sullivan while a woman in a party dress was singing. Sal walked to the television and turned the dial until the woman looked like an idiot with her big smile plastered across her face and her hands out to the side like whatever she was singing was important instead of being just a song.

"Broadway," his father said. "Where's that, anyway?"

"New York," Sal said.

"That's what they say, but that's just so we keep listening." His father stared at the television as if he could make the woman stop breathing with his mind.

"Where is it, then?" Sal said.

"Heaven," his father said. "You know—where the walk-on-water crowd lives."

The woman on television disappeared, and Ed Sullivan hunched forward like he did when he talked, giving the name of a man who stood in one place and only moved his lips, so Sal knew he was a comedian. Sal wondered if he was funny, but he looked too old for that, older than Sal's father. What could be funny when you were old?

Sal's father poured the fresh beer into his glass and swallowed half of it. "You watch out for that crowd, Sal," he said. "Your mother thinks she's doing you such a big favor sending you to the Angels School, but your life is here in Chicago, not in the clouds."

Sal nodded. He could hear his mother saying, "You're all we have." He was the only person he knew in school who didn't have brothers and sisters. It was so strange he'd decided his father's sadness began there because other than that his house was like everybody else's.

MARY

Sister Bernice hurries to her desk and lifts the key from the top center drawer where she keeps her seating chart. Mary turns in her seat and looks at Sal because Sister is rushing back to the doors and there's no chance she is paying attention to anything as petty as note passing. The smoke is already thicker when she opens the first door. Mary swivels almost completely around, looking past Vincent Ruzomberka's big square head to watch her unlock the outer door, carefully open it a crack, and slam it shut at once. Sister Bernice closes the inner door as well and says, "We have a fire, children. When the alarm sounds, we won't be able to go out the way we always do during drills. We'll have to wait for the firemen to put up ladders for us to climb down."

"Is the fire in the hall?" a girl in the front row asks.

"I'm afraid so," Sister Bernice says, and just then they hear the alarm bell, and everyone watches Sister Bernice as she sweeps toward the windows. "Stay seated," she says. "This isn't a drill."

SALVATORE

Sister Bernice backs up to a window and peeks out into the school yard, but Sal already knows exactly how far it is down to the cement—twenty-five feet. His father told him that when he'd moved upstairs in the Angels school building for fourth grade. "You'd break your neck jumping from those windows," he told him, as if Sal were thinking about jumping to show off to his friends.

Sal's father had parachuted into France on D-Day. He'd been wounded, but only after landing safely. Sal remembers his father explaining how to land softly when you parachute. The secret is relaxing and letting your knees take the shock. Sal knows that he was born because his father was sent home after he was wounded. If his father had been killed, he wouldn't exist; if his father had escaped injury, he would be somebody else in the seventh grade.

It's a funny thing to think about, and Sal is pretty sure he doesn't have it exactly right. Mary has three brothers and two sisters. All of them go to Angels, one in every grade but fourth. Sal imagines what it's like in her house with so many people. He is nearly certain it would be easier to talk to her if he had brothers and sisters. Sister Bernice lifts a long pole and un-latches the high locks on each window. She pushes all of them up as far as they go, and nobody says a word about how cold it is.

"Stay in your seats until the firemen arrive, children," Sister Bernice says after she replaces the long stick in its holder. "Let us pray for them to get here quickly."

Everybody bows their heads, but Sal keeps his eyes open and sees Angela does too. He opens Mary's note and reads, "Will you walk me home after school? It's only half an hour until then, almost no time at all. I promise I won't change."

ANTHONY

"Anthony Vicaro," Sister Veronica says as every fifth grader packs into the aisle by the windows. He regrets trying to act cool by being the last one out of his desk because he's in the back of the crowd, and it's easy for Sister to lay her hand on his arm.

She leans so close he feels her breath on his face. "Ciga-rettes," she says, and he shakes his head, remembering the mint, but even when she coughs from the smoke, she doesn't take her eyes off him.

She doesn't know for sure, he thinks. She isn't God.

He pulls away and shoves past a group of girls until he can reach for a windowsill. When he climbs up, he hears Sister Veronica say, "Anthony, it's too high." He shrugs like an eighth-grader holding a cigarette and grips the window frame more tightly.

SALVATORE

Sal remembers his mother before she complained aloud to him. It's only been three years, as if when he turned ten, he was someone for her to confide in, as if she'd been waiting for his birthday like it meant his ears were old enough for listening. Like he was a priest, Sal thought back then, and right away he tried to forget thinking that before God overheard him.

Sal has looked at pictures of her from five years ago, and she looks happy in all of them, but so does his father, who he's never seen smile except in these photos, as if seeing Sal turns his father anxious and grim, worried that there's something about Sal that proves he's failed at more than becoming a foreman or opening his own shop.

"Your father brought his limp home with him in more ways than one," his mother said one day last summer. "It gives him privilege, so he thinks. You know *The Red Badge of Courage.* You know that story?"

Sal said no, but she went on. "If there was a second book, your father could be the soldier coming home and expecting heaven to knock on his door instead of the other way around."

Sal knew she'd read the book in high school because she'd never read anything but *Reader's Digest* since he could remember. He wanted to ask her what grade she'd been in when she read it, but he kept quiet and let her finish. "Your father was so careful," she said. "He thought that if he did everything right he'd come home in one piece, but the boy next to him tripped a mine, and you know the rest."

"Most of it," Sal said, giving her an opportunity to keep talking if she wanted to.

"That other boy, your father told me, was opening his canteen while they walked across a field. That boy wasn't watching for a second or two, and then he was gone just like that, and your father suffered too. He'll never tell you that story, but you'll hear it anyway from time to time. He'll say whatever you do, make sure you don't have to rely on anybody but yourself. That's how that story's told now."

"OK," Sal said.

"Your father acts like he wants you to follow in his footsteps because he's ashamed to tell you otherwise, but don't let him fool you," his mother said. "Your father would lay down and die for you. Loving you isn't his problem."

Each night when he cooks, Sal imagines his mother dead. It would be just like it is now, he decides. His father would still sit in front of the television. He would still sip beer as he watched in the dark. Sal hopes that he is right because every other future he thinks of is worse.

"You'll get your turn," Sal's father said last week, pointing to his leg while news about the Soviet Union was on television. "Nobody will use the bomb. Nobody's that crazy, but they're all crazy enough to use what they always have, and that means they'll need you."

"I hope not," Sal said.

"You sound like your mother, like somebody who's a wisher." His father waved at the screen and said, "Turn that down for me, would you?" before he went on. "Everybody thinks we'll be fighting the Russians, but that'll never happen. Both sides have too much to lose. You'll end up shooting at somebody from a country nobody's ever heard of where the people don't have a damn thing."

By now Sal can hear a noise he thinks is the fire. Sister Bernice asks for sweaters to stuff under the door, and three girls give her theirs, but when she gets close to the door, she coughs and doubles over, dropping the sweaters into the smoke. A girl stands up to pound her on the back, and John Guardino gets out of his chair and pushes himself up on the windowsill. A second later, another boy joins him. "Wait boys," sister says, moving back to the windows. "See? There are the firemen." She coughs again, and all of the students get up and push toward the windows. There is so much smoke now that everybody is coughing and trying to get their heads outside.

The noise from the fire is so loud Sal thinks it is in the room somewhere. "Stay calm," Sister Bernice says, "the firemen just have to get the gate open before we'll all be saved." When she asks them to bow their heads again and pray where they stand, only about ten of the girls look down. Angela turns to Sal and says, "Sister doesn't know what to do."

Sal understands that she's right, but he can't think of anything but the smoke and the noise that must be the sound fire makes when it gets huge. When he looks past Angela, Mary is near the window where Sister Bernice is standing. He nudges two girls out of the way and follows her, Angela right beside him.

MARY

Mary sees that only boys are in the first row. Two of them are tall enough to easily swing themselves up on the windowsill beside the one where John Guardino is sitting, but both of them stop there, looking down like they're stuck at the top of a Ferris wheel.

She hears Sal say, "Come on," to the air between her and Angela, and she watches him raise his right forearm and press it lightly against Angela's back. When Angela moves forward, Mary moves, too, before Sal's left arm can touch her.

More girls get out of their way. Two smaller boys whose heads barely reach past the windowsill step to the side, and finally Mary can see into the school yard. It looks exactly like it does every day at 2:35. Empty and a long way down. Mary thinks John Guardino will break both legs if he jumps.

SALVATORE

"The firemen are coming in," Sister says, and everybody pushing forward shoves Sal against Mary's back. He reaches up to steady himself, his hands on her shoulders. Her hands are on the windowsill. The firemen can't get the gate open. Sal hears coughing and crying from behind him, and he leans forward to get better air, his chin nearly on Mary's shoulder. Sister says, "Be patient," and one of the boys on the second windowsill jumps, screaming when he hits the cement, rolling over and holding his leg. John Guardino heaves himself out, pushing Sister Bernice's hands away, and jumps. When half the students left in the room begin to scream, the pitch is so shrill that Sal can't tell the difference between the boys and the girls.

Sal leans out and sees John Guardino lying on the cement, one leg pedaling. There are already three boys from other rooms on the ground, one not moving at all, but a fourth is standing, hopping on one foot and then sitting down. The boy who climbed up beside John Guardino is holding on to the side of the window, blocking the way.

The firemen bash a ladder against the gate where it's held together with a lock, and one of them swings a sledgehammer. One of Sal's friends jumps and lands with a grunt. He crawls on his hands and knees for a few feet and then curls up in one spot crying.

MARY

Mary can hear screaming from other windows. "There," Sister says. "There they are," and she sees the firemen rushing through the gate. "The firemen are here," she says, "praise God," but everybody is coughing so much no one answers.

They have ladders, and one of them is propped against the windowsill that she and Angela and Sal are farthest from. It will take, Mary thinks, a long time to get all of us down that ladder.

She remembers that the air is better near the floor, but by now the smoke is so dense the only place to breathe is by the windows. She sees Sal pull his shirt up over his mouth and nose, lifting it loose from where it's been tucked into his dark pants. The fire sounds as if it's above them, which seems so strange that Mary thinks she must be wrong.

There are men in regular coats below them. From the neighborhood, Sal thinks. Fathers. Night-shift workers or men who work Saturdays and have Monday off. His father is three miles away in a machine shop working on something made of metal. The last time he'd been there was when his mother had dropped him off just before his father's shift had ended during the summer. "You want to work there like your old man?" his father had said while they were walking the twelve blocks home.

Sal was rubbing something that felt like sand off his bare arms. "No," he said.

"It's good work," his father said. He sounded disappointed, as if he'd expected Sal to be as excited as he'd been back when he was nine and gone to the shop with him for half a day. "Your hands or your brains," his father said. "Your mother will be happy when she sees which way you're headed."

By the time six classmates have been rescued, Sal sees both boys and girls jumping from the window in the room next door. One of the girls is on fire, and Angela tries to scramble up on the sill. Sal pushes her from behind, one hand on her rear end. She will only be going fifteen miles an hour when she hits the ground, he guesses, trying to remember his father's formulas.

MARY

Mary sees one of the men in a topcoat rushing toward a place below their window as Angela crouches on the windowsill. Angela reaches back for Mary's hand just as Sal pushes from behind. She tumbles off the sill head first. Mary leans out and sees the man break her fall with his body, both of them collapsing to the cement.

A fireman rolls a screaming boy who looks like he's burning up. He pats the flames down and starts up the ladder again. I have to jump now, Mary thinks. She hears a series of explosions and looks behind her to see the light fixtures disintegrating.

ANTHONY

Anthony Vicaro feels himself being lifted off the windowsill by a pair of arms. "Come on, son, let's move now," the fireman says. Anthony looks up as he descends. Sister Veronica is leaning out the window as if she wants to ask him a question. When he reaches the ground and scurries away from the building, he hears screaming from every upstairs window. There are so many voices his breath catches, and he begins to cough.

SALVATORE

All of the men who are dressed like his father in the school yard are begging somebody to jump. Sal pulls the boy who won't let go back into the room. "Jump," he shouts at Mary, "Jump," his voice skidding up into falsetto as he begins to lift her. Sal sees Mary's thigh appear, white and smooth. He is so close he could touch it by moving his hand six inches. Sister Bernice reaches to tuck Mary's dress down as she swings one leg over the windowsill. Vincent Ruzomberka jostles against Mary, and she is thrown to the side, spun so she is facing the door before she falls. Sal pushes up, brushing against Sister Bernice's habit, and he lifts her up beside him. She is lighter than Mary, he thinks, and he hears her saying, "Forgive me, forgive me, forgive me," as he swings her off the windowsill.

As Sister Bernice tumbles to the ground, the ceiling collapses, the room turning into fire that explodes toward the windows. Sal feels its brilliance surround him. The light follows Sal as he falls, his knees flexed to cushion his landing, his arms inside his burning shirt flung outward for balance.

PERFECT

AFTER ALBERT SWANER CONFESSED TO killing six young wom-
en in fourteen months within fifty miles of us, Cassie saw his
picture in the paper. "Oh, my God," she said. "It's him. Trivia
man—PSCORE."

I knew this had something to do with the trivia game Cassie
played at the two nearby bars that were linked to a national
broadcast of questions. CountDown, it was called. At Damon's
I'd sat with her once after sharing wings and cheese fries, and
I'd watched her answer five questions, four of them so quickly
she scored one thousand points for each one before a set of
commercials began. By the time the next set of questions came
on, I was watching a football game on the big screen next to
the one that showed the questions. By half time I was ready
to leave, but Cassie, even though she'd played three games by
then, showed no signs of losing interest. "You met him?" I
said.

She told me Albert Swaner had sat beside her two months
ago after she'd posted a good score in Vartel's, the local bar that
carried the game. "He was nice," she said. "He was fit looking
for a man in his late forties. You could tell he exercised."

It struck me as peculiar how she was remembering him in

such a way, and I said as much. "OK," Cassie said, "I'll tell you what I didn't like about him. Every time PSCORE punched his answer in, he reached for his beer like there was no chance the other clues would make him change his mind."

"That's it?" I said.

"Isn't that enough? Don't you get it?"

She turned angry, and I'll admit I was interested in what I considered larger issues—whether Swaner had found one of his victims in Vartel's or, at the least, how many other women were telling a similar story that morning.

I didn't offer up my curiosities. I knew an error in judgment when I saw it swaggering into the room, and I was ready to confess it was some news to get, much more personal in its "narrow escape" than, say, coming up on a jackknifed tractor trailer seconds after it's whipped into a compact car carrying an unlucky family. Cassie, though, couldn't seem to get over it. The very next morning, a Saturday, she drove to the library and read about each of the killings in back issues of the city newspaper, bringing me the news that every one of those women disappeared on her way home from a bar, though none of them, it turned out, was our Damon's or Vartel's.

By that time, because I always came over to her apartment on Saturdays, I was sitting on her couch, the television tuned to a pregame show for college football, something Cassie clicked off to get my attention. "He didn't bury them," she said. "He left them where they could be found by accident. He wanted ordinary people to find dead bodies."

Just then, listening to such a recap as that, I did my best to be who Cassie wanted me to be. I wrapped my arms around her and listened to her curse Albert Swaner until she started to cry. And before the next week ended, I read four of those accounts myself, noticing that Cassie, though she brought up the case all three nights I showed up at her place that week, never acknowledged that the women were always naked when found. "Bodies," she said, as if that covered it, but I thought she was right to think Swaner got a second jolt of pleasure when he read about who it was that found each of his victims—a hunter, two boys, an old couple who hiked to watch for birds, and best of all, most likely, another young woman jogging.

By the following Saturday, she was into analysis. "Maybe I was smart enough that he let me live," she said. "Maybe he picked women who got lousy scores because he thought they were too stupid to live." The television was on mute, the first game of the World Series, something that didn't need volume, but I wasn't having any trouble keeping my eyes on Cassie. "He congratulated me when I got more than twelve thousand," she added. "I remember his exact score in the next game, the one he played sitting beside me. He had thirteen thousand seven hundred fifty. He missed one answer, but he didn't change it."

"I don't get it," I said.

"You lose 250 points if you have the answer wrong when the round ends," Cassie said. "Didn't you pay attention that one time I played while you sat there?"

"No," I said, there being no reason to lie once I gave up my ignorance.

"You can get partial scores all the way down to small numbers by switching your answer when the screen posts the third clue, the one that gives the right answer away. I've never seen anyone get more than fourteen thousand, and he would have done it if he'd switched." Cassie was pacing now, holding her rum and Coke so carelessly I thought she'd tip the drink onto her carpet. "There must have been a dozen players, but nobody else at the bar got over eleven thousand on that game except for me just making it with him sitting beside me like that. And when they put up the bar's high scores, PSCORE had the four highest ones. I remember because they were all higher than thirteen thousand seven hundred fifty. And all the other ones had odd numbers, so I knew when he played by himself, he didn't drink beer after his answers like that."

She took a sip from her drink and started pacing again. To slow her down, I said, "He didn't meet them playing trivia. I've never seen women playing by themselves."

"What do you know? You hardly ever go into Damon's. You've maybe been in Vartel's twice. I can't be the only one."

"It's called a representative sample," I said, though I knew I was taking the wrong tone.

"You know what I remember now?" she said.

"What?"

"When he missed that one answer, he said the game was wrong. That there was a mistake. He was more than two thousand points ahead of anybody else, and he said that. He got negative two-fifty and blamed it on a lousy fact checker."

"It was short for Perfect Score, wasn't it?" I said.

"His name? Really? You think so?"

"I'd bet on it."

"I never think of any name but CASSIE when I play. It feels like I've been giving up my phone number now."

***

I had things of my own that worried me, most particularly how the company I worked for had all of a sudden announced it was shutting down, sending me home for good before two weeks more had passed. We made furniture—quality pieces—but it seemed as if people bought either high-end or cheap, dreadful stuff made of second-rate wood or even particle board. We did mostly oak and cherry, and I found out, before those two weeks were up, that there wasn't another furniture maker within two hundred miles.

I needed to reconsider who I was, and right about the time Cassie was fretting about Albert Swaner, I'd temporarily become a house painter–slash–deck reconditioner, sprucing up the outside surfaces of houses owned by people who could afford to not take on such jobs themselves.

But October was already on its downside, and that line of work was skidding away like daylight savings time. I started asking around, getting a feel for what might be out there. There was no way, I told myself, that I was going to check the want ads, the part of the paper printed up just for the ignorant and the desperate.

Meanwhile, as Swaner faded from the newspaper, he resurfaced in the tabloids, and then, in the real magazines you can't find by the checkout counters in the grocery store, what I discovered when Cassie brought one home and showed me. "Look at this," she said. "Can you imagine?" but she didn't say another word until she'd finished it.

"All the women graduated from college," she said. "Two of them had masters degrees."

"How did he know?"

"They must have told him," she said. She propped the magazine up on the cluttered night stand beside her bed. The first object she could make out when she wakes up in the dark, I thought. I was sure there would be a book on Albert Swaner within a few months, and it would include pictures of the six women, photos of Albert Swaner as a child. "I told him I was magna cum laude," she said. "I remember joking that all of my studying had bought me second place in a bar game and giggled like some idiot who'd get seven thousand for a score because she hardly ever got an answer right until the third clue gave it away. I wanted him to like me."

"You need to put this aside," I said. "Swaner's out of the running. He's where he's going to be forever now."

"I won't go in Damon's or Vartel's by myself. Not to play that game. Not ever."

"I'll go along to keep you company," I said. I was feeling generous. It was an easy thing to offer.

"Really," she said. "And when I get home? Then what?"

"I can stay," I said, fighting down the eagerness in my voice. "I can move in if you'll have me."

Cassie looked me over as if she was considering the difference between me sleeping with her on weekends or every day of the week. "I leave a light on all night in every room now," she said. "I don't think you even noticed last weekend."

"You can turn them off now."

"No, I can't. If there's only one for a killer to put out, I'll be in the dark right off. With four lights on different switches, I'll know someone's there before the second or third one goes out."

It didn't make much sense to me, but I slept just as well with the lights on full blast, and I told her so.

***

Once I started staying over every night, I sat beside her from Monday through Friday to watch *Jeopardy*, the game that gives nerds a chance to show off. It turned out there was a guy who'd been on for months. "I thought you had to quit after a week?" I said.

"Not anymore," she said. "Not for a while now."

Cassie called out her answers so fast and accurately I told her she could beat the guy who never lost. Three of those first five nights the other contestants were mathematically eliminated before Final Jeopardy. "You think those people are terrible players, but every one of them could do what I'm doing," Cassie said, shutting off the television before the audience stopped applauding. "I knew all fifteen answers once in CountDown, and I still got 13,772 because I hesitated a few times, read the list of answers all the way through to be sure."

"You're safe," I said. "He's gone for good." I leaned in to kiss her, flinching when the television suddenly roared back on, a commercial for fried chicken, the volume set loud like it had been so she wouldn't miss hearing a question.

"Sorry," she said, flicking the chicken into darkness. "My finger was still on power, and you made me press it."

Lots of people meet serial killers and live, I told her then, or else we wouldn't be able to keep up with the slaughter. And think of all the people who went to high school with them or worked in the same office. I told her something I'd read about a woman who danced with a serial killer, but she thought the writer was making it up. "He'd have killed her if that was real," she said, and then she clicked on the television again, turning to the news station as if she expected to hear about Albert Swaner's escape.

A woman was describing the ups and downs of the stock market. Behind her, there was a graph that showed how the price of crude oil was rising. "You could be doing something yourself, and I'd never know it," Cassie said.

"Doing something?'

"Killing."

"So could anyone," I said, though I knew that was an awful answer.

"That man Swaner had a wife," Cassie said. "Can you imagine?"

* * *

I was thinking of giving up my own place, how maybe this Albert Swaner thing was a sign and a way to hedge against the discomforts of being unemployed, moving out of my own apartment for good. It was something to consider while I painted, easy work, because I mostly did the wide open spaces on the houses. There were two guys who did trim and narrow spots, the painstaking stuff, places where a homeowner might check to see if he was spending his money wisely. A temp guy like me could hardly fuck up large panels unless he was drunk or high. Or unless he loaded up his brush like a little kid and let globs run down the side of the house to harden into scars.

It took my mind off Cassie a bit. Though when a good-looking woman walked past a house we were working on, there was always talk about tits and ass and how they'd look out in the open if somebody could sweet talk her into undressing right there in the yard.

* * *

So everything settled for a bit, the weather holding through a long stretch that guaranteed me hours, Cassie not seeing anything new about Albert Swaner in a newspaper or a magazine, her even turning off the bedroom light, content with the ones in the living room, kitchen, and bathroom to keep her from harm.

Until she plugged a new night light into a bedroom socket one night, and I asked her what was up, whether she'd lost a step on her way to recovery. The light gleamed near the door, but with the overhead light on in the living room, it looked to me like uselessness itself. "Did you know there were men in India who used to strangle women because of their religion?" she said.

"That's something I never heard of."

"You Google serial killers, and there's so much to read you'll never finish," Cassie said. "It's not just Ted Bundy and the Hillside Strangler."

"Those men sound worse than Albert Swaner. They sound like guys who think the worst things they do are for the better."

Cassie shook her head as if she knew those killers. "They said the victims were sacrifices for the goddess of terror. They buried them and poured sugar on their graves. They were nicer than Albert Swaner."

I didn't see how the dead would make distinctions like that. It's the living who decide what's preferred, and always without knowing firsthand. "You know what sugar always stands for in those stories," I said, coming up with a lame one-liner like that because her story had brought up the willies in me.

Cassie shook her head again. "Don't be stupid," she said, but she let me unbutton her blouse, and I didn't hazard another one-liner until she was wearing just her bra and panties. I looked at her in the bedroom mirror from behind, my hands unhooking that bra. We watched as if the two people in the glass were in a movie, her breasts and my hands belonging to someone else, and when she was completely naked I shuffled around to face her, surprised when she raised her hand to her mouth and stepped back.

"What?" I said, but without saying anything she tugged my shirt over my head, worked my pants to the floor, and pushed me down on the bed, kneeling above me. I loved watching her breasts as she straddled me, but when I pushed up to kiss them, shifting my weight, she pressed both hands against my chest, worked herself onto me, and moved against me so wonderfully I closed my eyes, keeping them shut until both of us shuddered and moaned.

I opened my eyes when she didn't slide off. She was staring at me in a way that made me feel like I was on film. "I can't be underneath you," Cassie said.

"OK."

"Not ever." Her eyes moved over my chest and stomach, and then she pushed up and stepped away from the bed. "I never watched your face before," she said. "You don't look like yourself with your eyes closed."

"You looked strange yourself back at the beginning," I said, working up something to say besides "What the fuck are you talking about?"

"When was that?" Cassie said. She had all her clothes in her hands, holding them in front of her.

"When I finished undressing you, I thought you were going to stop or something, and then you practically tore off my clothes."

"Oh," she said. "It was just a weird flash," and she backed into the bathroom and closed the door.

I heard her arranging herself, water running, the medicine cabinet opening and closing. It took her maybe five minutes to come out again, dressed and smiling. "There," she said, but she didn't come close to the bed where I was still naked with the sheet pulled up to my waist. For a moment she looked like somebody I'd paid, a woman ready to leave after she'd done her job.

"Going somewhere?" I said, keeping my voice light.

"The living room," she said. Her hand was on the door in a way that made me think she was going to close it when she left.

"What did you mean, 'weird flash?'" I said then.

"I was afraid when you were dressed and I wasn't," she said. "It was like you were somebody else."

"OK," I said, "who's that?" though I wished at once I hadn't added that because I thought she meant Albert Swaner.

"Nobody special," she said, "just not you." And then she was gone, not stopping in the living room, but walking into the kitchen where I could hear her pouring water into the teakettle and placing it on the stove.

I picked up the magazine with the article about Albert Swaner and read it. "We started to think there was a karaoke connection," a detective said. "All those women but one sang the night they were killed. Those bars all had karaoke. We staked out on those nights, and all along it was that game. I never heard of it before. If we'd thought of it sooner, we might have put a stop to it after two or three were dead."

When Cassie came back with two cups of coffee, I said, "We need to go to those bars. Get you over this business."

"I'll do Damon's," Cassie said, "but never Vartel's."

"You need to do both," I said, but she shook her head.

"You don't understand," she said. "There's more where he came from."

"Yes," I said, "but not so many you have to worry. There's always lightning, but you don't look up."

I stopped myself when I saw her expression shift to rage. I glanced at her hand that was wrapped around her mug and expected her to toss her coffee in my face. "I met the future," she said, "and I didn't recognize it."

* * *

The next night, at Damon's, we sat in the nonsmoking section of the restaurant. We ate appetizers—quesadillas and spring rolls—and Cassie said she was stuffed. She shifted sideways on her chair and stared into the bar where maybe twenty people were sitting. I thought she was watching the screen that was showing CountDown until, turning toward me, she said, "I'm going to stand up now like I'm ready to leave, and you tell me which man at the bar is examining my body."

She stood before I could tell her I wouldn't be a part of this. "Nobody is," I said at once. "Not like you think."

"He won't look away, Jack," she said. "He'll be the guy who keeps staring even when I turn toward him." She shifted away from me, and I followed with my eyes, glancing past her, but every one of the men at the bar did nothing but sip their drinks while looking at sports news or CountDown.

"Nothing," I said. "Nobody."

"I should leave," she said. "If I walked out of here, you'd see who it was that wanted to follow me."

***

The next morning, a Saturday, Cassie folded the local paper over and handed it to me at the breakfast table. "Check this out," she said, and I was relieved to see it was an article about a nearby farmer who had converted his cornfield into an enormous maze.

Another day without a mention of Albert Swaner, and better yet, this corn maze sounded like fun, something we would have maybe tried weeks ago if we'd known about it. "It's raining," I said, "but the forecast for tomorrow is great."

"So you want to go?" Cassie said.

"Why not?"

"There will be lots of kids there," Cassie said, as if she still needed to convince me. "Families."

"Tomorrow," I said. "For sure."

The last Sunday in October was as sunny as the weather man had predicted, a day to be outside, but the change back to Eastern Standard Time meant it would be going dark by five o'clock. "You know what this is like?" I said, the two of us entering the corn maze just behind another couple.

"A metaphor," Cassie answered at once. She was looking from side to side, and I thought, because we could see people passing by us on adjacent paths through the stalks, that she was checking to see if anyone, man or woman, was going through the maze by themselves.

"An old board game. Uncle Wiggly. You ever play that?"

"No, I didn't. I was an only child. I didn't get to play board games."

I wanted to tell her about the rabbit trying to find his way home, but I remembered that Uncle Wiggly was a hand-me-down from my mother, a game maybe, that hadn't been sold for years. I was already feeling disappointed because we could see those other couples and families through the stalks. All of them were talking, ruining the effect. "Follow me," I said. "I think I know how to make this harder," and after we deliberately took right and then left and then right turns to work toward the center, we didn't see anyone nearby or run into anyone coming back along our path. "Just like I thought," I said. "This is better."

"Somebody must stay out here in the dark," Cassie said. "Like for a joke."

"Their car would be parked in the lot," I said. "Anyway, they'd have to make sure the field is empty before it gets dark." Cassie was suddenly glancing around as if she was about to panic. "There's a sort of lookout thing over there where we started," I said. "A platform. Somebody's job is to get up there to check."

"Oh," Cassie said. "That makes sense," but she was looking through the stalks on either side as we walked. When two minutes went by without anyone passing near us, she stopped. "It feels like we're really lost," she said.

"Good. That's the idea. It wouldn't be fun if it was too easy."

"No," Cassie said. "It feels like we're not in the maze anymore. It feels like we're just walking between rows in a field where nobody else is."

I touched one of the blue ribbons that lined the path. "The stalks are still tied back."

"To make us think we're going to get out."

That night I found those killers Cassie had told me about on her computer. They were called "the Thugs." It said they mutilated those women after they killed them. Cassie couldn't have missed that part. It was right before the paragraph about pouring sugar on their graves.

* * *

The next day the rain returned at noon, a downpour with no sign of letting up. "Go home," Jack Wuerfel said. "Or follow me to Vartel's for some afternoon delight."

He was the boss, so everybody laughed. "Lost in the Seventies," Larry Foss said from where he'd been sitting in his truck cab listening to the radio for half an hour. Only Wuerfel laughed. Foss was just another guy with a paint brush, and nobody else seemed to get it, and I knew this was because they were the only guys over forty.

I didn't need to piss away an afternoon drinking, though I figured I had time to stop at the mall to look at CDs. I wanted to surprise Cassie with something bluegrass, something sad but full of hope, but before I reached the FYE store, I saw Cassie walking in front of me. She didn't notice me, I was sure of that, and I started to close up the distance until, just as I passed the CD store, still ten or fifteen steps behind her, I slowed down enough to follow her without letting her know I was there.

I passed Spencer's Gifts, The Gap, a pretzel shop and the CVS drug store. That's all. You could verify how little time I kept pace with her by walking past any four stores at a mall. How long that is. How you might measure me. But I admit someone watching me would know what I was doing, just like seeing a man holding a book in the sex section of Barnes & Noble, you know everything about what he's thinking except which sex he longs for.

Not even a minute, that's for certain, but I'll own that I enjoyed watching Cassie walk like that unawares. It made her seem like she was an attractive stranger, a woman whose breasts and waist and hips and legs I admired.

If she ever asked me about how I saw women I know I would lie. There wasn't a way to explain that pleasure without making her feel like a "beautiful cunt," what Larry Foss called each of the best looking women who passed while we painted. I was beginning to think I wanted her to love me, and I thought if I was consistent in my lies, she might even trust me as well. In order to stop that sort of thinking, I called her name and quickened my steps, turning her into someone I knew.

We had all afternoon to ourselves, and that meant the new bluegrass CD followed by sex, but this time, after she straddled me like she had every night for the past two weeks, I took her shoulders and rolled her over. "You need to get past this," I said, but she began to struggle, and I slipped out of her, then slipped back inside as she squirmed. "Oh," she said just once, when I came quickly, and she pushed me off so I lay beside her, both of us breathing heavily, then calming, neither of us speaking because something had happened that needed to be assessed.

What a rapist must feel, I thought, and then I said, "What an asshole," to myself as if self-deprecation was a synonym for decency. Cassie had curled up, pulling the sheet over herself. She looked like somebody who was working up the courage to call the police.

* * *

The second week in November brought four consecutive sixty-degree days with cloudless skies. "One last job before I have to let you go," Wuerfel said the first morning. I nodded. I knew the fortunate streak of weather was responsible for an extra week's pay. I'd been watching the weather channel regularly for six weeks now, gauging my work schedule, and I knew a front was due Monday night or Tuesday morning, thunderstorms followed by blustery winds and a temperature drop into the low forties or upper thirties, far enough down to make the forecaster predict a mix of rain and snow for Tuesday afternoon.

As it was, the light began to fade by 3:30, and by 4:00 we were off our scaffolds, the temperature dropping quickly despite the low sun, all of us turning on our headlights for the drive home at 4:30.

Tuesday morning, at seven o'clock, the first of the thunderstorms hit. The weather map on television had a white cloud that signaled snow just a state to the west. Behind it, the temperature color represented thirties across half the country. I gave myself the rest of the week to enjoy before Monday made me start looking for a winter job.

"It's too late to be Santa Claus," Cassie said. "He comes to the mall tomorrow." When I didn't smile, she added, "The warehouse is looking. I saw the ad in the paper."

"Wright's? Night shift?"

"Good," she said. "You already saw it."

"Not really. That ad runs every day. That's not a good sign. It's like those Help Wanted signs in every fast-food restaurant. The signs never come down, so you know it sucks there."

Cassie pushed the paper toward me, and I was ready to slap it away, but it wasn't folded over to the want ads. Instead, the story running down the right hand column was about the first victim of Albert Swaner, a graduate student named Kristin Ault. "First of a six-part series," it said, and I read the five paragraphs down to "continued on page 8" and stopped.

"Don't throw this away when you're done," Cassie said.

"All right."

"And don't spill something on it. Read the sports while you're eating."

"I get it."

"That prick," Cassie said. "That goddamned conceited prick." She pulled the newspaper toward her and smoothed it out. "If we go to Vartel's tonight, will you play trivia with me?"

"Sure," I said. "I'll call myself Professor. That way nobody looking at me will guess I'm the one who sucks."

"You can only use six characters," Cassie said.

"OK. I'll be Prof. People will still get it, won't they?"

* * *

After five questions, I got the hang of it, using the clues to up my chances for choosing correctly among Meryl Streep, Katharine Hepburn, or Elizabeth Taylor as the woman with the most Oscars for Best Actress. After fifteen questions, the top score was 11,982 for DEEK, followed by 11,765 for NONAME, what Cassie was calling herself. On the screen, four more names followed before the list said PROF and 8390. Three scores were worse than mine, including someone named BLITZ, who had a score of 190, and I thought of a child or someone stupid with beer. "He probably stopped playing," Cassie said. "People do that. Leave in the middle."

She stopped as if she was trying to hear what the two men with game keyboards were saying at a nearby table. I listened, too, before I said, "You'll be OK now. It's good you came back to Vartel's and played again."

"Albert Swaner wouldn't have left in the middle, if that's what you're thinking," Cassie said. "He'd have finished the game first so he could post a score. I bet he never killed a woman who quit and left."

"What's next?" I said.

"We play again," Cassie said. "We try to do better," and I nodded and stood up, practically jogging to the men's room to piss away the pitcher I'd nearly finished.

Three men followed me in, two of them leaving before me because they didn't stop to wash their hands. The third, as I started to wash up, leaned over the urinal as if he had to concentrate on his target. When I reached for a paper towel I noticed a scattering of fingernail clippings in the sink. Someone not long ago had stood there and clipped his nails before returning to the bar. There were full, thin crescents and short, sharp bits, and I turned the faucet again, running water over the fingernails to wash them down the open hole in the sink. As they swirled away, I thought I saw a group of dark, short hairs, as if that man had also trimmed a mustache or a goatee, something you might do in a bar's men's room if you were meeting a client or a woman.

I reached down to guide them into the pouring water, but they turned out to be small scratches in the surface, as if the sink had been repeatedly clawed. When I slid my finger across them, I touched a clipping that hadn't been swept away, and

I felt myself shiver, pulling my hand up so quickly I looked around to see if the man at the urinal was watching.

I came back to Cassie with a smile, and she scored 12,270 for NONAME, first place, and PROF moved up two spots with a 9,885. "You're getting better already," she said, but I could see that one of the players who had scored 11,000 had stopped playing.

"You're so good at this," I said, "you should play more often. Sooner or later you'll get 15,000." A round of karaoke had begun in the next room. A woman was trying her hand at "Wicked Games," a song so difficult, given its range, that I expected her voice to be wonderful. Cassie was fixed on the screen, and when the next set of scores appeared, I understood why. The high scores for Vartel's scrolled down, and I saw that NONAME's 12,270 was the second highest score, even though it was lower than what she'd earned that night with Albert Swaner.

"You were in the men's room when these came up before," she said. "Look at that. They must delete the scores after a month or so. His are all gone."

She was right. If PSCORE had played here again and filled every slot in the top ten before he was arrested, he hadn't done so in what looked to be the past sixty days. The karaoke singer was having trouble with the high notes Chris Isaacs had hit years ago like the reincarnation of Roy Orbison. "Oh, I don't want to fall in love—with you," she sang, faltering on the extended "I." They keep them current so there's a good chance somebody playing each night will make the list," I said. "The bar wants people to be happy for a few minutes."

I meant to comfort her, of course, or maybe even lift her back toward a place of balance from where she could see her good fortune. "But you know it's not the best. You could only believe that if you've never been here before." The song ended to applause that stretched on too long. Cassie was crying now. She looked like someone a man would sit down beside, that stranger leaning just a little toward her and saying, "What's wrong?"

"To think I never knew enough to be frightened when I was in here before," she said.

That's crazy talk, I caught myself thinking. Cassie sounded like somebody who would give up driving because a fatal accident was on the news, but I was examining the three men at the bar who looked to be drinking alone.

Only one of them was playing CountDown. I decided he was the player with the nickname LUVR. He looked miserable; his score had been lower than mine both times. There was no way he could be a copycat killer.

The other two were staring into the bottles behind the bar, both of them in the middle distance of concentration on getting drunk. It was impossible to foresee murder here, and I told Cassie that in the calmest voice I could muster.

"Yes," she said, but then the screen flashed an announcement that the next game was about to begin. I was ready to tell her I'd play until sunrise, but the screen declared that the next game was called WipeOut, and Cassie swiveled on her stool, turning her back to it. "I hate that game," she said. "It's just like CountDown, only there aren't any clues. You either get a perfect score or you get nothing."

"OK," I said, holding her coat so she could slide her arms into the sleeves. When we stepped outside, I breathed in the air like a man welcoming winter. Across the street, a design seemed to form in the brick wall of an apartment building. "Look at that," I said, pointing and crossing to the opposite sidewalk. "See?"

I shouted back to Cassie. The way the bricks had lost the mortar between them looked like the letters ZLZ, as if the building housed a fraternity or someone had taken the time to pick the mortar out in the secret acronym for a gang. I laid my hand on the bricks and traced the design as if I could sense something, a way of reading the building's mind. For a moment I felt that if I pulled at the bricks, I could work them out of the wall and create a stencil of absence someone could be pressed against in order to be branded.

"Get over here," Cassie said, her voice barely audible. Though the street was empty, she looked like she had that night in Damon's, and I shut up and took her hand. Her car was parked two blocks from the bar, and though the rain had stopped and the car was just four spaces down the side street, it seemed to be settled deep in gloom. Even then, I didn't think about the danger of walking there until I felt Cassie tighten her grip into the unmistakable pressure of fear. I began to swivel my head from side to side, checking for movement. "It's darker here than in the country," she said, and though I thought that wasn't true, I said, "Maybe."

"All these people and so little light. It doesn't make any sense."

"They're asleep," I said. "It's Tuesday, and it's late."

"It's not that late. Someone should be up."

"I'm sure they are," I said and felt her hand tighten again, gripping me so hard as we approached the car that I glanced up at the windows nearest us, sliding the key into the lock without pushing her hand away.

"That's what I thought, too," she said. "Doesn't that terrify you?"

ROGER THAT

Roger Wharton, the man who lived next door, recited the names of all the vice presidents in order: William King, John Breckenridge, Hannibal Hamlin, Andrew Johnson. He was a whiz. Schuyler Colfax, Henry Wilson, William Wheeler, Chester Arthur. The only time Pete Logue and I knew Wharton wasn't making up those names was when a president got assassinated and somebody we'd heard of took his place.

"Roger that," Pete Logue said when Wharton finished up with Lyndon Johnson.

"Before you have your dads buy you encyclopedias, you come talk to me," he said, moving on to the categories for books in the Dewey decimal system while we finished the Cokes he'd opened for us in his kitchen.

And as soon as school ended in June, Pete Logue and I, the only two boys on our street between the ages of eight and fourteen, did just that, drinking his Cokes while we listened to him recite on Wednesday and Saturday afternoons. I was eleven, Pete was almost thirteen, so neither of us could do anything but spend time together unless I wanted to play with seven-year-old Jimmy Meenan or Pete tried to make friends with fifteen-year-old Victor Hutka, who had sideburns, a mustache, and a car he drove without a license.

Roger Wharton lived by himself in a house that stood between mine and Pete's. "He came with the neighborhood," my father said. "He and his wife, Susan, in that big house with no kids to use it."

My mother had explained, once, that the Whartons had moved in when they were still under thirty, expecting children and then, when they didn't arrive, stayed on, filling their eight rooms with souvenirs from traveling during the six weeks Wharton took off each summer from his job. "His dental practice," my mother said, a strange way of putting it, especially since our whole family was his customers.

We'd lived on Cranberry Street since the year I was born, four years before Susan Wharton had died in a car accident, falling asleep at the wheel a thousand miles from that house, her husband walking away, my father said, without a scratch when they were broadsided on the driver's side. Seven years now he'd been alone in that house, so his wife was a photograph to me.

"It was after his wife died that he started to come up with all these lists," she said. "It's like since he stopped traveling, he had to collect something, so he started in on whatever he could accumulate."

"Something he doesn't have to cap or clean or polish," my father said. "Something he doesn't have to take care of. Nobody needs to know these things." He drove a truck, spent a hundred nights a year or more sleeping somewhere else. "I know the names of the roads when I see them; I know where they go. Wharton couldn't find his own back door in the dark."

"He's an educated man," my mother said, looking out the kitchen window at Wharton's weed-filled, uncut lawn, the burned-out shrubbery he hadn't replaced since I could remember. "It's not in his nature."

"He's long ago gone to seed," my father said, and that was the end of it until the next time my father noticed one more unkempt thing in Roger Wharton's yard.

He didn't seem to know that Wharton's shrubbery looked better on the side of the house that faced Pete's room. It was all rhododendrons over there, which I took to mean they were hardy and needed no care to blossom every May while half the azaleas on our side had failed and worse, the junipers had overgrown and split, parts of them sagging and brown, the rest of them towering green above the roof line. My father, looking from our porch, said he thought Wharton must feel guilty every day when he saw his yard looking like a mouth full of cavities, something you couldn't get anymore unless you drank Coke and ate candy all day.

What I never mentioned to my parents was that the tone of Wharton's voice changed when he was reciting lists. The rest of the time he sounded like a dentist, like someone who knew the secrets you kept. I thought about how he could see how careless I was about brushing my teeth, that I never flossed.

His dentist voice was the kind that sounded like a grandfather, like a man used to seeing others, even adults, as children. But when he did lists, he sounded like a kid. He never sounded like a man his age, like a father, Pete's or mine or anybody's I knew. It was what made me think, sometimes, that my father was right to dislike him.

* * *

"Listen to this, boys," Wharton said one afternoon as we drank Cokes in his living room, the two of us sitting on his couch while he pulled a chair up close to face us. "Collective nouns. You know what they are?"

We both got that look that comes with not doing homework the night before an oral quiz. "A school of fish," he said, and we nodded.

"Everybody knows that one," he said, "but try these on. A pace of asses. A shrewdness of apes. A knot of toads. A bale of turtles."

We waited, but that's as many as he listed. Pete shrugged, but I was enthralled. *A shrewdness of apes*—who thought up this stuff? And where did Wharton find it?

"Roger that," I said, because these were exactly the things I wanted to know. The only weird list of things I knew was all the letters for Morse code, the dots and dashes from a to z. I'd been in Boy Scouts for six months. Pete had quit two weeks after I joined, and by now he couldn't remember any letters except the dot for e and the dash for t.

"Boy Scouts," he said the week after he quit. "Have fun."

But he had to admit Wharton was infallible. Even when we picked the category, South American countries, instead of letting him decide, he named them from Argentina to Venezuela. We asked for the names of everybody on the Supreme Court, and he gave us a roster we had to trust, since we didn't know anybody but Whizzer White, an old football player my father talked about for two days when he'd been appointed the year before by Kennedy.

My favorite was all the bones of the body, the way Wharton showed us just where everything was located, having us touch ourselves in a sort of Simon Says of anatomy. "Pick a spot," he said, and we put our hands on our shoulders (clavicle) and near our eyes (lacrimal). We slapped our hips (pelvis) and our thighs (femur). "You could learn them all," he said. "There are only two hundred and six."

Pete put his hands behind his back and shoved one inside his pants. "Tailbone, right?" he said, keeping his hand there.

"Coccyx," Wharton said. "There's a real name for every part of you."

That was the day he walked us down the hall for the first time. "That's my weekend bedroom," he said, "and this is my weeknight room."

He didn't open either door. But there was a third bedroom that was full of the kinds of souvenirs I loved—multicolored, glittering rocks; slices of tree trunks smoothed and glazed; a hundred different shells, all of them larger than anything I'd ever dragged home from the beach. I'd been in dozens of shops that sold stuff like that, but all I'd ever been allowed to buy were postcards. One wall was covered by a bulletin board plastered with what looked to be fifty bumper stickers thumbtacked in rows, all of them with the name of a national park from Arcadia on the left to Zion on the right.

"I had a teacher once who had us memorize the national parks," he said. "I did it in one night and then had to wait two weeks to take the test. I'll bet you boys haven't been taken to ten of these so far."

"Roger that," Pete said, and I hoped Wharton wouldn't ask how many national parks I'd been in because the answer was zero.

***

Two weeks after school was over for the summer I had my annual checkup at Wharton's office. My mother drove me and waited in the lobby. "It's just a cleaning," she said. "You haven't had a cavity in three years. Why would you get one now?" I thought of all those Cokes, whether Wharton had a mouth full of cavities himself from drinking them when Pete and I weren't around.

Instead of reclining halfway like it always did, the chair tilted me back to nearly horizontal. I tensed, half gagging on spit even before anything got started. The dental assistant, who looked like she was just out of high school, had a tag that said Marie, and she stopped reading my old X-ray report when she heard me clear my throat.

She patted me on the shoulder. "Something new since you were here last," she said. She leaned close, her breasts so near to me without touching that I thought she must have practiced this in school, how to stand so that her breasts didn't brush against patients lying on their back. Someone had graded her, maybe, or at least given her advice.

When Wharton walked into the room, he was wearing a surgical mask and a loose green smock, but I could see the top of his blue tie and the collar of his white shirt. "How's that smile of yours doing?" he said through the material that was the same color as the smock.

"OK, I guess."

"You guess? Marie says it's perfect."

"OK."

"Let me take a look, just to be certain. Open."

He was done with me in a minute. "Good for another six months," he said.

"Roger that," I said to myself. I looked for Marie on the way out, but I didn't see her in any of the rooms. My mother smiled as she made my next appointment. "Perfect," she said as if she'd been consulting with Marie. "Thank you, Roger," she said then, and I turned to see that Wharton was standing in the doorway. He had his mask pulled down; it hung near his collar.

"My pleasure," he said.

"I hope I'll get as good a report next week when it's my turn."

"Of course you will," Wharton said. "You keep after yourself."

* * *

"What do you think a man does in a house alone?" my father said a few nights later as we finished the slices of pie my mother had served us.

"It would depend on the man," my mother said at once. She'd cut herself a piece of pie so thin it looked like an icicle on her plate. "His circumstances."

My father glanced at me as if we shared a secret. "You know who I'm talking about, don't you, big guy?"

"Mr. Wharton," I said, though I knew what my mother meant, that there must be millions of men who lived in a house alone.

"There," my father said. "Wharton. That puts a face on it. What do you think he does? He never has visitors. You never see him outside."

My mother pushed the pieces of her pie crust into a small pile that looked like something you'd put a match to. "He reads. He watches television. There's plenty to do besides entertain."

My father grunted. He liked to have people around when he was home. He'd invite other couples for barbeques or a group of men to play cards. "Who wants to sit around?" he'd say. "When you're not working, you should enjoy yourself. When I have the yard in shape, I want people to see it."

"He probably has hobbies," my mother offered.

"Hobbies," my father said, making the word sound like smoking or drinking or shooting heroin. "What hobbies do you think a man alone all the time has?"

My mother sighed, but she didn't answer. I went down both sides of our street, listing the names for all twenty-four houses, but none of them except Wharton's had a man living alone in them. "Reading," she said. "Reading's a hobby."

"Reading?" He looked at me again. "Big guy, you think all that reading you do is a hobby?"

"No," I said.

"See?" my father said. "There you have it."

"What do you know, Bill? It's possible a man can enjoy things that you don't."

"He's a man who does nothing is how I see it. When I'm home I have things to do here. Fixing things. A yard to tend to. Wharton either lets things fall apart or hires out."

"He's a dentist, Bill. He has the means. What would you do if you didn't drive half your life and work around the house the other half?"

My father had a thin smile fixed on his face, the kind teachers used when nobody knew the answers in class. "Danny's a visitor," my mother went on. "He and Pete are over there all the time. Roger's not a recluse."

"That's my point," he said. "That's my point exactly." He

pushed his chair back and stood without looking at either of us.

"Bill," my mother began, "you're wrong," but my father had his back turned by then, disappearing through the side door into the yard.

My mother gathered up the dishes and stacked them in the dishwasher. "Your father," she said. "Sometimes."

I nodded. I was sorting through all of the points my father could have been making, but none of them made me think, Roger that.

* * *

That summer, when my father was on the road, my mother started serving TV dinners. I loved them, especially the roast turkey with the stuffing that looked like a piece of bread turned brown by spices and the salty gravy. "You'll get them as long as you don't tell," she said early on, and I didn't. I knew my father despised food that came ready-made. Paying to have somebody do the work you can do by yourself is how he put it. My mother could cook, so why wouldn't she?

My mother would make one for herself and give me the meat and potatoes part after she acted, each time, as if she might eat the thin slice of roast beef or either one of the two small pieces of fried chicken. All I had to do was take my time and wait in order to get doubles of the parts I liked best. She'd eat the peas or the corn or the mixed vegetables and the little piece of cake or cobbler that came with each meal. "I'm always making a pig of myself when your father's home," she said. "He thinks people never change, that I was thin when he met me, so I'll always be thin. If he was home three hundred sixty-five days a year I'd turn into a big fat blimp."

I smiled when she said something like that because it meant the meat and potatoes were coming soon. TV dinners didn't have enough food "to keep a bird alive" my father would say, and he was right about that, but my mother would say, "For a man who's so fussy about everything, he doesn't tend to his own belly."

The first month of the summer my father made two one-week runs, and my mother fell into the habit of walking to Teresa Savage's house, eight doors down, to play cards after dinner. "Pete can come over, but that's all," she said. "I don't want you wandering around the neighborhood when I'm not home."

I didn't mind. She served ice cream with every TV dinner, never making a bowl for herself, but letting me slip a couple of spoonfuls in her mouth after I put chocolate syrup all over it. "Mmmmm," she said. "If I let myself scoop it into a bowl, I'd eat myself sick. Now you and Pete stay out of trouble."

Before she left, she always made a big show of throwing the foil trays away. "No dishes," she said. "That's a bonus. You run the rest under hot water and let it sit out. And you make sure all this goes in the trash before your father gets home and sees what we're up to."

***

One Wednesday afternoon in mid-July, Pete came out of his house with his hands behind his back. "I got something for us to do besides drink Cokes with Roger That," he said, and he showed me his father's rifle. "It's just a twenty-two," he said. "It's a pop gun."

I held it like I'd seen men carry a gun in the movies. I felt like I was guarding something, that I needed to keep an eye out for problems.

He put his hand in his pocket and pulled out four bullets. "What do you think?" he said. "Want to shoot at something?"

"What?" I said, looking at the trees across the street.

"Birds," he said. "You can blow a bird to bits with this."

It seemed like something neither of us could do. Birds were small and kept moving unless they were far away. "OK," I said, confident we'd be done in a couple of minutes, the four bullets used up. It was Pete who would be in trouble if his father kept an exact count of his ammunition.

I was right. By the time I was taking my second shot we'd missed three birds, and all I was thinking about was where my bullet had ended up because the bird I'd fired at was sitting on a branch above us, and there were houses a hundred yards away.

The last bird that looked like a target was on the ground fifty feet away. I was relaxed by now. Pete couldn't shoot worth a damn either, and when I pulled the trigger the bird flapped once, then righted itself and staggered a bit before hopping. "You hit it," Pete shouted. "Jesus, look at it."

He walked toward the bird, and I had to follow. It looked as if I'd nicked its wing, turning the bird clumsy. We were ten feet away, but all it did was run. Except through a window, I'd never seen a bird from this close, and I was suddenly terrified, handing the rifle to Pete and letting him stand over the bird, a robin, as it slowed down.

I wanted it to fly, but only one wing opened. I didn't need somebody's father to tell me that bird was going to be killed by something before too long.

Pete spun the rifle around his finger like it was a baton, and it slipped off onto the ground before he could finish a full circle. "I got it around twice in my room," he said. "It looks so cool."

The bird had settled now, like it had given up. "Your Dad's going to be pissed, isn't he?" I said.

"I'll clean it," Pete said. "I watched what he does. He'll never know, and I only took four bullets. There's no way he's counting that close. Dads never know anything unless you're dumb. Your dad's the same way. You could get away with anything if you tried."

"No, I couldn't. He's always checking up when he's home."

"That makes it even easier," Pete said. "You only have to be good when you know he's coming." Pete picked up the rifle and twirled it again, finishing a circle before it caught and dangled. "See?" he said. "I'm going to practice until I can end up with the gun pointing at something when it stops, something cool like that." He looked at the bird and the surrounding trees as if he was searching for more targets. "I still can't believe you hit it. How cool is that?"

***

Two nights later, when my father came home before dinner, we went to one of the drive-ins my father loved. There were seven of them within twenty-five miles of our house, and all of them showed movies we could have seen indoors three months before, but my father said movies were meant for places where he could relax after he'd been driving for a week. What that meant was he could bring a cooler full of beer and a bag of potato chips, but my mother never complained, and neither did I because she always bought us Cokes and popcorn from the counter beside where the bathrooms were, and we watched with him until the second feature ended.

In July that meant 1:00 a.m., yet there, when we came home, was Roger Wharton walking back to his house. He was wearing shorts and a tight t-shirt that made him look as skinny as Pete and I were, but nothing clicked because I was groggy with near-sleep, until my father said, "What's he been up to, you think?"

My mother said, "Who knows?" but my father left the car running and nobody opened a door while Wharton, without looking our way, crossed his yard and entered his house. "A man needs to be trusted," my father said.

"You can't expect everybody to be like you," my mother said. "That's not fair."

"There's fair and there's necessary, Arlene," he said. "You get to choose, but a man on foot this time of night is something I'd call odd."

"More people should walk," she said. "Half the world is fat these days."

"You want three guesses and see if you don't start thinking what I'm thinking?" my father said.

"Bill," she said. "Save it for later."

"Maybe I shouldn't," he said. "Maybe it would do some good to talk out loud."

He turned the key then, and I followed the two of them into

our house. When I heard my father talking in their bedroom, I was too tired to go to their door and listen.

* * *

Pete sighed, but he still went along on Tuesday when Wharton called us over after he saw us in Pete's yard. It felt different being in Wharton's house after supper, and we hadn't been there ten minutes before I had to use the bathroom. When I came out I could hear Wharton talking to Pete in the kitchen. "How many animals that went into space can you name?" he said, for once not listing them.

Pete said, "There was a dog and a monkey, for sure. A chimpanzee, too." He sounded like he was in school, like he was bored and was looking at the clock just before it said 3:15.

"Yorick was first. We sent him up. And then Patricia and Mike. They were all monkeys of one kind or another, and we recovered all three. And then the Soviets sent up Laika. Remember her? The dog? The Communists just let her go around and around until she ran out of air and died."

"That's the only one I ever heard of," Pete said. I could tell he was ready to leave. He'd been complaining about Wharton since July began, sounding the same way he did about Boy Scouts six months ago.

"Gordo," Wharton said. "Sam, Belka, Strelka."

I tried the doorknob of the weekend room, and the door swung open. I kept listening for Wharton's voice while I looked inside. It was full of pictures of Wharton's wife. In the living room, the pictures were of him and his wife together, but here she was by herself in every one—a wedding picture, a couple where she was even younger. As Wharton kept talking, I tried to guess which picture had been taken last, narrowing it down to two in fall foliage that didn't look like trees from anywhere near our street. She'd died in October. The day before, I thought at once, or at least no more than a week before. They might have been developed after the funeral when Wharton picked up the camera and found a used up roll of film inside. I closed the door and tried the knob of the weekday room. The door was locked, and I began to sweat. I was sure the other room was meant to be locked as well, that if Wharton knew I'd opened it, he'd never speak to me again.

I finished my Coke and we left. By now it was nearly dark. "I'm glad he doesn't get to look in my mouth," Pete said. "Molars, bicuspids, incisors, or whatever. What's he doing right now, you think? Memorizing the stars?"

"That's impossible."

"No, it's not. There's always some weirdo who knows something nobody else does. There has to be a map. You know, with names on it."

"Who would name all the stars? There's a gazillion."

We both looked up at the same time and immediately looked down. We laughed then. "Roger that," Pete said, but a moment later he was wearing his angry face again. "Anyway," he said, "what kind of dentist has a refrigerator full of Coca-Cola?"

"He gives it to us," I said. "Maybe he doesn't drink it."

"Get it?" Pete said, sounding exactly like my father at the dinner table, like he knew something I didn't but I was expected to learn.

"My dentist doesn't want to be friends," he said at last, and because the only thing that came to mind was "Why not?" I didn't answer.

"My dentist has us sit up in a chair," Pete added.

"He just started," I said, regretting the story I'd told him about Marie and the new chair. "Maybe he's just trying it out."

"What's a man think about when he has a woman half lying down like he does all day?" Pete said. "I bet he takes his time with their teeth; he gets an eyeful if he has a mind to."

I knew what Pete meant. I thought of Marie, the assistant, and what she would look like lying on Wharton's dentist chair.

"Mrs. Starrett goes to Wharton for her teeth, and she's an eyeful," Pete said.

"Yeah," I said. I'd heard Pete's father say that all the time about the woman who lived on the other side of Pete's house. She'd just been married. "What an eyeful," Mr. Logue would say when she crossed her yard. Even when her husband was walking beside her, Mr. Logue would whistle under his breath.

"Your Mom's an eyeful," Pete said. "You don't notice because she's your mom, but trust me, if you were somebody else, you'd think so too."

I thought of the pictures of Wharton's wife, trying to decide if Pete would think she was an eyeful, but when I wasn't in Wharton's house, I didn't think about asking Pete, and he never said a word about her.

* * *

My father was sitting on the porch when I got home, and he noticed me in the doorway. "Bring me another one of these, would you, big guy?" he said.

I carried the beer outside and handed it to him. "Have a seat," he said, smiling. There were three empty bottles standing beside his chair, which was unusual because my father was the kind of man who slid his returnable bottles into the case he kept in the garage as soon as he finished each one, a habit I thought he'd acquired so either my mother or I didn't count how many beers he'd had.

"You getting along?" he said.

"I guess."

"You're getting towards grown-up. I come home and I hardly recognize you sometimes."

"That's good, isn't it?"

"Six of one, half dozen of the other," he said, and he took a long swallow of beer.

He pointed his beer at Wharton's yard. He looked like he was thinking about digging up the dead bushes and taking the mower to the lawn. It was the look he'd give my room when the bed wasn't made and there were board games and clothes on the floor. The look that started my hands moving. He'd cleaned up one time when I was eight. He'd made my bed while I sat in a chair and watched, tugging the blanket so tight it looked like a board, and then he'd picked up two handfuls of model cars and thrown them in the trash. The only thing I did right that night was refuse to cry.

"Is it a mess inside?" he said.

"No."

"You sure about that?"

"Everything looks clean."

"I've got half a mind to check for myself," he said. "It doesn't follow from what I can see."

"Trust me," I said.

My father didn't shift in his chair, but when he didn't say anything for a minute, he looked different, like Richard Hoak looked when his report card said he'd failed fifth grade, changing into somebody I wasn't going to know anymore.

"There's limits, Denny," is what he finally said. "You and your mother both need to learn that." He picked up the empties and carried them into the garage. When he didn't come out, I thought he'd opened a warm beer in there, that he was drinking it fast before he stepped out again and went to the refrigerator for a cold one.

I heard the screen door groan, and my mother, holding it open with her elbow, said, "What's that father of yours doing with himself in the garage? He's been out here forever already."

I threw up my hands and tilted my head like I'd seen actors do in a hundred TV shows when they pleaded ignorance, but my father reappeared before she could ask another question. "You're leaving again tomorrow," she said, "and here you are mooning around out here half the night."

"It's my job," he said. "What do you want me to do?"

"It's more than two weeks this time," she said. "You have a boy who's almost twelve. You know what that means?"

"You bet, Arlene," he said, lifting her arm and brushing past her. "You bet I do."

My mother didn't follow him. She caught the screen door with her hand and held it open like she expected me to come inside. I sat in my father's chair and looked at Wharton's raggedy bushes for almost a minute until I heard the door close.

* * *

By the time I got up the next day, my mother had gone to the store, and she served TV dinners for lunch, something new. "I bought you a whole slew of them. Your father's going to be away for a long haul. Teresa's invited me for bridge. I know it's a Wednesday and the afternoon, but things don't always have to be the same. I want you to promise to stay right here like it's night." She squeezed my shoulder. "Help yourself to a bowl of Neapolitan," she said. "That will get you started, and then ask Pete to come over. I haven't seen you and him together much lately. Did you forget how to use the phone?"

I watched her walk down the street until it curved and made her disappear, and then I ate three scoops of ice cream, washed out the bowl, and waited ten more minutes before I headed over to Pete's house. I had a couple of hours before she had any chance of finding out I'd left the house, and if she called, I could say we were watching television and didn't hear the phone, which was in the kitchen.

Mrs. Logue waved as I came through the back door without knocking like I always did and turned down the hall. When I walked into Pete's room, he was standing at the window with his back to the door. He was staring so hard I thought I could touch him before he heard me, and I tiptoed halfway before he said, without turning, "Either stop there or get ready for this."

"What?" I said, hurrying up beside him.

Wharton's weekday bedroom was on the side of the house where the rhododendrons had gone halfway up the windows, but from Pete's room we could see right in, and there was my mother kissing Roger That. The bushes cut them off at the waist, but as soon as Wharton's hands went underneath my mother's blouse, lifting it so I could see her bra, I sat down on

Pete's bed and stared at the clock radio, waiting for the minute number to flip over from three to four.

"It's OK," Pete said. "I've never seen anything. You can't see from here except when they're standing up."

The four dropped into place, and I pulled the radio toward me, yanking the plug out of the wall. I wanted to throw something, but Pete said "Whoa," and I just held it stuck at 1:44, the numbers dark but still visible.

"It's not my fault," Pete said. "I didn't want you to know unless you found out for yourself."

***

My mother went to Teresa's for cards three nights while my father was gone. Each time I hurried to Pete's house to make sure he was watching television instead of my mother. His parents watched with us like they always did, but when Mr. Logue walked down the hall like he was going to the bathroom while commercials were on, I counted 1,001; 1,002; 1,003; imagining him slipping into Pete's room for an eyeful before I got to 1,100.

The day my father got back, my mother had dinner on the table, but he just opened a beer and said he wasn't hungry. "I ate fast food at one o'clock," he said. "Two Big Macs fill you the hell up. I need to wash the road away."

After my mother and I ate the battered fish she'd fried, I followed her out to the porch where my father was sitting beside four empty bottles. "I have half a mind to clean up that yard of Wharton's while I'm home," he said. "It keeps me from enjoying even one minute out here seeing that mess."

"Relax, Bill," my mother said. "By tomorrow you'll be ready to take care of your own things." She handed him a fresh beer, but my father didn't lighten.

"What do you think, big guy?" he said. "There's always the names of the books of the Bible to learn, right? Genesis, Exodus—there you go, you can finish them off just like that."

"Bill," my mother said.

"It's a hobby," he said. "Leviticus, Numbers, Deuteronomy. See?"

I thought of Pete Logue watching Wharton undress my mother, and I wondered if she had ever been completely undressed before she disappeared onto the bed. For sure, Pete had seen my mother naked from the waist up.

"Seashells, driftwood, and lots of colored stones," I said, and my father looked at me. "That's the start of a list of things in Mr. Wharton's bedroom," I said. "You should see all the stuff he has in there."

"What sort of man has boys in his bedroom?" my father said, staring at my mother.

"Moccasins, belts, and a whole shelf of key chains," I said. "There's hardly any space except on the bed."

My mother looked stricken, but I knew there was no way, even though she was the only one of us who knew what was in Wharton's weekday bedroom, she could correct me.

"You know what I'm talking about, Arlene?" my father said, but my mother just shook her head slightly. For a moment, just then, I was ready to say I'd seen all those things from Pete's room, that I'd never been in any of Wharton's bedrooms, but my father was so angry I began to add all of the pictures of Mrs. Wharton, the ways in which she was dressed, the swim suits she wore. It didn't seem like lying. Even if nobody slept there, all of those items were in bedrooms.

My father stared at me. "You trying to tell us something?" he said. "Is there something we need to know about this god-damned dentist?"

I glanced at my mother, but she had an expression that reminded me of the one on that wing-shot bird. The only way I could stop talking was to run down the hall to my room.

As soon as I threw myself on my bed, I heard my mother say, "No, Bill," but then the front door slammed, and I popped right up to see my father appear in Wharton's yard, shouting for him to come out because they needed to tend to some business right this minute.

Wharton, when he stepped outside, said, "What's this about, Bill?"

"You know exactly what it's about," my father said, taking two steps forward, closing up the distance between him and Wharton, who stiffened, but didn't step back.

"No, I don't, Bill. You'll have to tell me," Wharton said.

"Your bedroom," my father said. "You get my drift?"

Wharton looked over my father's shoulder, and I knew he expected to see my mother in one of our windows. Maybe, in fact, he expected her to call out to my father, asking him to come back inside. I waved so he would see me, and when he looked back at my father, he turned into Roger That, explaining about the ways he was helping me learn. "I have a lot of things a boy likes to look at," he said. "I thought you'd appreciate it, Bill, you being away so much. Curiosity, active learning, association, metaphor."

"What's he talking about?" my mother said from behind me somewhere. I hadn't heard her step into the room, but when I didn't turn, she came up close, laying her hands lightly on my shoulders so I knew she was looking across the lawn at the two men she slept with.

My father hit him then. He drove his fist into Wharton's stomach, folding him up. My mother clutched my shoulders as Wharton wheezed, making a noise that sounded like Pete's dog whistle, something imagined more than heard.

And then my father looped a roundhouse right and caught Wharton flush on the ear, spinning him into the spotty azaleas. "You stay away from my family," my father said. "Understood?"

My mother stood behind me then. "It's OK," she said. "I promise."

* * *

In my room that night I saw Roger Wharton's hands under my mother's blouse, the way his face had pushed between the cups of her bra just before I turned away. Breastbone, I said to myself, though even I knew the real name was sternum, something that seemed made up so doctors could learn the bones without thinking of the body parts they wanted to touch.

What list had Wharton reeled off for my mother the first time she was in his house? There were thousands of lists, but none of them, I was suddenly sure, were something a man would tell a woman he wanted to undress. It would have to be later, when they were dressed again, when they were in the living room with all of that junk that cluttered Wharton's shelves and tables, getting in the way of the pictures of him and his wife. The names of dentist tools. The names of healthy foods.

My mother would listen like I did. She would remember parts of those lists even if she didn't give a damn about any of them. And then the idea that he would recite a list to her sounded so foolish I knew he'd never say a word about the animals in space or the vice presidents, that those lists were his hobby, what he did when he was alone or in the company of boys.

ABOUT THE AUTHOR

GARY FINCKE is the Writers Institute Director and Charles Degenstein Professor of English and Creative Writing at Susquehanna University. Winner of the 2003 Flannery O'Connor Award for Short Fiction, the 2003 Ohio State University/*The Journal* Poetry Prize, and the 2010 Stephen F. Austin Poetry prize for recent collections of stories and poems, he has published twenty-seven books of poetry, short fiction, and nonfiction. He grew up near Pittsburgh and currently lives in central Pennsylvania.